Constarry Crossing

After witnessing something he was not meant to see, Major John Stearman should have died on the ferry on the Constarry River.

Now, two years later, he is still trying to put the events of that day behind him. But it seems others cannot let it lie. Someone is hunting down the witnesses of that fateful day, picking them off one by one.

Major Stearman must turn hunter himself, before he, and someone he deeply cares for, become the next victims on the killer's list.

Constarry Crossing

A. Dorman Leishman

A Black Horse Western

ROBERT HALE · LONDON

© A. Dorman Leishman 2015
First published in Great Britain 2015

ISBN 978-0-7198-1619-2

Robert Hale Limited
Clerkenwell House
Clerkenwell Green
London EC1R 0HT

www.halebooks.com

Typeset by
Derek Doyle & Associates, Shaw Heath
Printed and bound in Great Britain by
CPI Antony Rowe, Chippenham and Eastbourne

CHAPTER 1

A thirsty horse took John Stearman to the Constarry River that day, a neat, long-legged chestnut mare called Bella. She had been with Stearman for almost two years and since they had both come through the recent conflagration relatively unscathed, he intended keeping her.

She had taken a minie ball meant for him, as well as a sabre slash to the chest, and had cut her fetlock pretty badly leaping over a barricade to get him out of a desperate situation, with him clinging for dear life to her back. Once, when ill with a fever, while he lay in a fog of sweat and aching limbs, Bella had been commandeered by his colonel's aide. As soon as he found out, Stearman had gone to find her. He was scarcely able to stand but he was so angry that she had been taken from him while he was too ill to protest that adrenaline and fury got him as far as the colonel's quarters where he demanded the return of his horse and refused to budge till she was brought to him. Later the colonel would complain that Stearman had the damned effrontery to check that she was unharmed before leading her away. It was behaviour he wouldn't have tolerated in anyone else, but Stearman was his best officer, a man of infinite good sense, brute courage and with natural tactical abilities, not to mention that he was the best horse soldier he had; yet for the remainder of the war he would refer to him as 'that damned horse-thief'.

Stearman dismounted, loosened her girths and watched her step daintily into the shallow margins of the river, turning to look at him with soft brown eyes.

'Take your time, sweetheart,' he encouraged, and watched as she dipped her mouth to the water.

There had been a ferry here a year ago, the last time Stearman had passed this way. He and a couple of hundred other Union soldiers had been in retreat from an advancing Rebel army. It was a fairly calm and orderly retreat that had allowed them the luxury of using the platform-and-pulley ferry to get everyone across a river that had been broad and too deep to ford for a dozen miles on either side.

Stearman couldn't believe what he was looking at now; the river was shrunk to a mere stream, the riverbed of boulders, gravel and sand exposed and dried out. Further downstream he saw the remains of the ferry, the ropes cut, the platform marooned on a sand spit. There was no evidence to show what had happened to cause the diversion: something further upstream, he supposed. There were cliffs on the north side of the river, about six miles away. A landslide maybe.

He had fought and killed his way across this land for four years and now a piece of paper had been signed and it was all over, hard though it was to believe. He had shaved off his cavalry moustache, got drunk with his best friend Sergeant Coopersmith and turned for home with Bella, newly purchased from the quartermaster.

Stearman wondered what had become of the ferryman and his family, for there was no living to be had here now. He turned to look towards the ferry house they had occupied but, as he was now standing on what had been the riverbed, his view was obscured. He climbed away from the river, Bella raising her head to watch him. He needed one or two supplies and maybe the people in the house could help him, if they still lived there.

The house that came into view was just as he remembered it: a long, low, single-storeyed structure, the roof cedar-shingled. His approach had taken him through the thin end of a stand of alders and just as he was about to step out of their cover, he saw activity at the door of the house.

Men in Union blue spilled out into the yard. They were dragging a man in a tattered, butternut Confederate uniform, gripping him by the hair, by his collar and arms, dragging him down the little path that led to a kitchen garden and then on into the trees where Stearman stood watching. As they pulled and dragged their prisoner deeper into the woods, shouting brutally and laughing and cursing at one another and at the Rebel, he followed them, keeping parallel, not showing himself until they stopped under a tree with a branch that looked strong enough for their purpose. Stearman saw now that they had a rope, that they meant to hang the Rebel prisoner. Quiet as could be, Stearman drew his sidearm and moved towards them.

But the hangmen weren't having it all their own way. The youngest of the five, a callow boy, no more than sixteen or seventeen, voiced his disapproval. Though he still had some growing to do, Hobie was already powerfully built, with broad shoulders and big hands, his blond hair long and tangled. His eyes had seen the grimness and tragedy of war but far from becoming embittered and brutalized by it, Hobie was determined to do no more than was necessary to survive.

'We don't hang prisoners,' he objected.

'We're hangin'' this one. Climb up there and tie off this rope like we told you.'

'No, sir. This is not right. He is a prisoner of war. We're obliged to. . . .'

The prisoner, on his knees, heard a beefy slap and suddenly the boy was on the ground, his mouth a mask of blood.

'Shut up, Hobie. Sergeant Parry said we was to hang him. That's all there is to it.'

The boy tried to get up but was abruptly sick in the grass and lay dazed for a minute, watching the trees and the men spin and tilt. They had the rope around the prisoner's neck now and were clumsily trying to throw the other end over the branch above his head. The boy came to a crouch and reached behind him for the Colt tucked into his belt. He fired one shot just above the cluster of men, not really caring if he hit any of them. The bullet bit into the tree bole and shot a splinter into the neck of one of them, Randall Anderson. He pulled it free, cupped a hand to the bleeding wound on his neck and cursed a stream at Hobie, who was looking incredulously at the blood on his hand.

'Hell is the matter with you, boy?'

The boy stood, his legs refusing to steady at first, till he pressed his heels down and his knees locked. He could scarcely hear himself think for the drumming of his heart.

'Take the rope off of him,' he ordered them, but directing his words mainly to the Rawl brothers, Luther and Nolan, almost identical though not twins, both with dirty blond hair, big jaws, blunt noses. Their uniforms were tight across the thighs and shoulders, but too long in the sleeves. Nolan was a shade taller; Luther had a scar under one eye, the only way to tell them apart. The other man, standing off to one side, was Phil Hunter, short, thin and pale; he looked like the war had taken a hard toll on him. In fact his lungs were shot and his body was struggling with a disease that was slowly killing him. The four men stared at Hobie, angry and baffled. The boy hadn't been with them long. He didn't know what was what. Maybe at first, in the beginning, there had been rules and give and take. Not now. Not after four years of seeing so many comrades dead at the hands of this prisoner's kind. You didn't turn your back on a dangerous opponent and give them another chance to kill you; any man who'd survived the slaughter of Fredericksburg would not deny that the Rebels were a merciless enemy.

But the boy had seen more than they knew and he wasn't about to put his soul in hock for one more unnecessary death, just because Sergeant-God-Almighty-Parry said so. He looked at these men, ragged and dirty, uniforms patched and mended and bleached with salt sweat. In the furnace of conflict they had been forged into something their wives and mothers simply wouldn't recognize, feral and bitter and angry and vengeful. Had they experienced a harder, tougher war than other soldiers to make them so pitiless and implacable? Maybe, or maybe they had been that way all along and war had just given them an outlet for a natural inclination towards cruelty. Had the war accidentally brought together six natural-born killers? Hobie had seen enough of what they were capable of in the last month to think that might be true.

'We don't hang prisoners. He walks,' he said firmly. 'Get going,' he told the prisoner as they lifted the rope from his shoulders. The Confederate soldier, a slender man in his forties, not very tall, pale-skinned, brown-haired, brown-eyed, took a step and stumbled on a tree root, took another step and then shouted something at the boy. Because his right ear was still ringing from that last blow from Randall

Anderson, Hobie heard the words too late.

'Behind you!'

The rifle stock hit Hobie on the back of the head and he went down, his finger on the trigger of his Colt firing a single shot into the ground as he fell. The wielder of the gun was Sergeant Parry, the man who had given the order to hang the Rebel. He was powerfully built, with black hair worn long on the collar, bright, hectic blue eyes, looked like he had a temper. He had been working his way unseen behind the boy. Now he looked up and jerked his thumb.

'Let's get it done,' he barked.

Stearman stepped into the clearing then and fired once at the sergeant who had struck Hobie, the bullet plucking at his sleeve and taking a thin slice of flesh with it. The sergeant gave a muffled yelp of pain and dropped the rifle. Stearman turned smoothly and fired again, over the heads of the other men. They froze, glaring at Stearman with anger and incomprehension. They saw a tall, well-built man in a Union Army uniform, his insignia that of major; he was close shaven, looking at them all with calm, interested, dark-blue eyes.

'Who the hell are you?' one demanded.

'Major John Stearman. I hate to break up your little party, but I have some news for you men. The war is over. He's not your enemy now.'

'Over?' Randall Anderson asked indignantly, 'How can it be over and nobody told us?'

'Lee surrendered three weeks ago. General Grant accepted his surrender at a place called Appomattox,' Stearman said. He looked at the boy on the ground, who was moaning, and starting to come round.

'Son of a bitch,' one the Rawl brothers said, shaking his head.

'It doesn't matter if the bastards surrendered or not,'

Sergeant Parry told them, one hand gripping his bleeding arm. 'That doesn't change a thing. There isn't a one of you hasn't lost somebody to these Southern murderers. This is just a little payback.' He turned full round to look at Stearman, his eyes hot with temper. 'If you know what's good for you, soldier, you'll keep your nose out of our business.'

'Business, you say? Burning and looting, killing civilians? This man is a civilian now. Or, if we're all still in the army, I outrank you, in which case. . . .' Stearman heard the sound behind him. Like Hobie, a second too late, he ducked and turned in the same movement. He had time only to glimpse someone tall and thin, dressed in dark clothing, before he suffered Hobie's fate. Something hard and unyielding was driven into the side of his head and he fell forward on to his knees. After the initial sunburst of light in his head, he surrendered to the darkness and lay still on the grass.

'Well, you don't outrank me,' this new man said, looking down at Stearman. He dropped the branch he had used as a weapon, and then raised his head and looked at his men. He was older than everyone else there, in his high forties, thin as a shin bone, a man the boy Hobie had come to look upon as without equal for viciousness and cruelty to all who crossed his path; a man without conscience, capable of the very worst atrocities.

'Did I bring you all safe through four years of conflict for you to let two men get the drop on you?' he barked at them. 'Where did he come from?' He jabbed a boot into Stearman's side.

'Just passing by, we figure,' Randall Anderson said. 'He said the war's over. Lee's surrendered. Fighting's over, looks like.'

The new man, a colonel by rank, looked at Randall as if he were the stupidest creature he ever saw.

'War ain't over, not this side of Christmas. If I hear any of you repeating that foolishness, you know what'll happen to you. Now, you've got five minutes to take care of this Rebel, then we can be on our way.'

He walked away then, seeming to want no part of the lynching, quite sure that his orders would be carried out, as they always were. His men had up to now followed his every word, slavishly, more than happy to do all his dirty work for him. But after young Hobie's outburst and the things this Major Stearman had said they seemed less enthusiastic. It was Sergeant Parry who rallied them; a man used to discipline and complete obedience. They knew what he was capable of if they didn't toe the line.

So they were finally going to hang the Rebel. They forced him down on to one knee, his head bowed under the pressure of Randall Anderson's huge hand gripping the back of his neck. Through his own hair, grown too long and straggling into his eyes, he could see the ferry house beside the river. They had set light to it, the flames were now combed to one side by a slight breeze, the roof snapping and spitting with the heat. As he watched, he felt his own heart being consumed by rage and despair. He had come all this way for nothing, survived everything the Yankees could throw at him for four long years, only to fail at the end. He hadn't expected his war to end this way. The prisoner kept his eyes on Hobie and Stearman all the while as the rope was looped and tightened. Until they hauled him up in the air and left him kicking, he kept his eyes on the two men who had tried to save him and had maybe died in the attempt.

CHAPTER 2

Stearman woke slowly, his brain struggling to make sense of what had happened to him. He'd tried to stop a lynching and had had his head stove in for his pains.

'Well, you're alive at least,' he murmured. His head hurt appallingly. It hurt at the front and back and behind his eyes and all the way down his spine. Dried blood had crusted one eye and had streaked a path down to his mouth and neck. He could taste copper pennies.

Slowly he began to take in his surroundings. He was lying on hard-packed earth but he was evidently inside a structure of some kind. It had a low, sloping roof about two feet above his head and wooden walls at arm's length; rough, unplaned wood, almost like bark.

He raised his two hands to the roof, which sloped downward from left to right, and pushed. There was no give, none at all. He tried to roll over or to put a shoulder or his back to it but there just wasn't enough room. He rolled back, trying not to panic. The inescapable fact was that he was in a coffin of some kind and already he sensed that he was breathing his own stale breath. The darkness pressed in on him like a physical weight and his panic tried to cut loose.

Deliberately he slowed his breathing, made himself relax

and slowly and methodically began to explore the wooden sides of his prison and its strangely canted ceiling. He found gaps in the walls and beyond that there was more hard-packed earth. He was in the ground, buried alive and his air was running out. He was going to die down here in this fetid darkness, after surviving four years of absolute hell; he was going to suffocate, unseen and unmourned after enduring Antietam and both battles at Bull Run. Through his mind ran visions of the things he had started to believe he would enjoy once more, hot baths, clean water, real food and the people he had hoped he would see again, his father, his aunt and cousins, and Clare, his sweetheart. They would all be lost to him, and they would never know he had been on his way back to them.

In desperation, he tried to bend his knees to force the lid upwards, but he couldn't get enough purchase and, for a horrible few seconds, one of his knees was trapped in the bent position, till he wrenched it free and lay gasping, his heart hammering.

'Sweet Jesus, not like this,' he murmured.

Then from above him a voice spoke. It seemed to be fairly close.

'Hold on,' it said. 'I'll have you out in a minute.'

There was a scrape of metal on wood, a thud and then the coffin lid lifted and cool air rushed in over Stearman. He took two or three deep gulps of it and blinked up at a famil-iar face. He realized it was the boy Hobie leaning over him. Hobie reached down, gripped Stearman by an arm and hauled him out of the root cellar he had put him in some hours ago. It was just a shallow trench dug into the ground, against the back of the barn, a little distance from the burned ferry house. It had a heavy sloping door, which Hobie had fastened with a rusting hasp because he didn't want Stearman coming to and wandering around, alerting the others to the fact that he wasn't dead, like he was supposed to be.

'Are you all right, sir?' he asked, crouching down beside him, his voice scarce above a whisper. Stearman looked groggily about him, at his 'coffin', at the boy and up at the night sky.

'How long was I in there?'

'Eight hours, about. How's your head? Can you walk?'

'Think so.' He got up slowly, his initial dizziness quickly passing, and found he was able to follow Hobie, who headed for the river at a low, crouching run, glancing back now and again to make sure Stearman was with him.

They crossed the shallows at a slower pace, so as not to splash and make too much noise, making for a belt of trees on the other side. Here Stearman sank down against a thick tree trunk, holding his pounding head, feeling the burn of nausea in his chest. Hobie sat down beside him, watching the river for signs of pursuit. He had a canteen over his shoulder, which he uncorked and handed to Stearman.

'Sorry, it's just water, sir. I figured you'd be thirsty in there. I brung some food as well, if you're hungry.'

Stearman drank the water gratefully and accepted the waxed wrapper of bread and cheese, but put it aside for later.

'I'm supposed to be on guard duty so I can't stay long, sir,' Hobie said.

'Can you tell me what happened?' Stearman asked. Hobie grimaced.

'They hung him, sir. They went ahead and hung him.'

Stearman sighed and shut his eyes for a minute. 'Well, we tried, Hobie.'

The boy seemed surprised that he remembered his name. He relaxed slightly, stretching out on the grass, his weight on one elbow.

'My real name's Walter, sir; Walter Hobart, but everybody calls me Hobie.'

'I'm very glad to meet you, Walter, more than I can say,' Stearman bowed his head formally to the boy and Hobie laughed quietly.

'You know it was Colonel Bell that hit you, with an old tree branch. I was just coming round myself and I saw him. Then he told the others to get on with it. We all went back to the ferry house after that, carrying you with us. Then the Colonel told me that I had better shape up or it would be the worse for me. He didn't allow no deserters in his unit. Murderers and thieves and . . . and other things, but not deserters. Well, sir, my folks didn't raise no stupid children. I apologized right off, said I was sorry I'd behaved like I did, said they could count on me from now on.' He turned away from watching the river and looked directly at Stearman. 'Colonel Bell told me to kill you and bury you and then I could get my supper.'

Stearman gave a short laugh, which hurt one side of his face and turned his laughter to a groan.

'So instead, you put me in the root cellar.'

'They went downstream a little ways to make camp. So I fired a shot in the air, dug up some dirt from another part of the yard and made it look like a new grave, then put you in the cellar.'

'I wish I'd had you with me at Bull Run.' Stearman grinned at him. Hobie coloured up and bent his head in confusion, clearly not used to praise. He pulled up some grass and twisted it around his fingers.

'They've had it all their own way long enough,' he said bitterly, 'But you have to get away from here now, Major, while you still can.'

'What about you?'

'I gotta stay a little bit longer. If I run now they might figure out I didn't kill you and then the colonel would make them track us down. He'd like that. I'll be all right, sir. I've survived this long.'

'How did you come to be with them, Hobie?'

'I'm a deserter, sir,' he said bluntly, after some minutes. 'I got word my grandpa was sick, so I just turned and headed for home, had enough, hadn't been paid in two months, had a hole in my boots and a busted rifle, so one day I just went in the opposite direction. We'd seen some pretty fierce fighting that day, lot of dead soldiers everywhere, so I figured they'd probably just think I was dead too. I met up with them,' he jerked his head towards the river, 'two days later. I was hungry and nearly lame in my foot, so they took me along with them. I didn't realize till later that they were deserters too, renegades, out to get whatever they could take. I saw them kill people, civilians, old folks, anybody that got in their way, and burn down houses, and take girls into barns and . . . and you know what. They tried to get me to join in but I never did.'

'Is that what happened at the ferry, Hobie? Was there someone in the ferry house?'

It took Hobie a minute to answer, then he jerked his head as if he would shake off the pictures in his head. 'There was a lady in the house, an older lady. Colonel Bell and Sergeant Parry stayed behind with her, while we took the Rebel into the woods. That's the way it always was. They'd take the women off somewhere while the others took care of any menfolk. I admit I ate some of the food they took and I stole a rifle, but that was all I ever did, and I waited for my chance to get away from them. But today – today was the finish of it for me. I've got no stomach for lynchings.'

'This Colonel Bell, he's the leader?'

'Yes, sir. I never met anybody enjoys killing like he does. Him and Sergeant Parry and Phil Hunter are the worst. The others are just along for the ride. That reminds me, Colonel Bell took your horse.'

'Funny, her name's Bella,' Stearman said. 'That's a pity. I've had her for two years nigh on. Meant to take her home with me. I bought her too, fair and square,'

He sighed and rested his head against the tree behind him.

'Wish I had my saddlebags. Had nearly a full bottle of bourbon in them.'

Hobie flushed and fidgeted with one of his frayed cuffs.

'They had that before supper, sir.'

Stearman sighed and said, 'Ah well.'

'Randy said you told them the war's over. That right, sir?'

'All over, Hobie.'

'Is that where you were going, sir? Going home?'

'I was. Home to my family, not to mention a girl who's been waiting for four years. Got my discharge a week ago. And you can go home now too, son, put all this behind you.'

The boy nodded, once to Stearman and once to himself. That was what he intended to do.

'I live with my grandpa and my aunt Mary. Got a little place just outside of a town called Dansing. We work pretty hard but we have a nice little house, there's always plenty of good food and my folks are decent, good people. Not like them.' He nodded towards the river. 'I don't know how anybody could get to be that mean. Randall Anderson is the only halfway decent one of 'em.' He rubbed a dirty hand over his face and gave a sigh that came all the way from his boots. 'Sorry, sir, but I have to go now, before they miss me.' 'All right, Hobie, but I wish there was something I could do to thank you for what you've done for me,' the major said, impressed by this young boy's character.

'No need, sir. I was happy to do it, more than happy.'

Stearman held out his hand and Hobie shook it with an honest, powerful, strong grip, then he got up and started back towards the river, but paused and looked back.

'Good luck, sir. I hope you get home safe.'

He gave the major a perfect salute, which Stearman returned, and then walked off into the trees. Stearman watched till he was completely out of sight, then he sank down on to the grass at full stretch, resting his aching head on his arm. His head hurt too much for him to go anywhere. He just wanted to rest a while, and then make a plan of some kind for the morning. He didn't think Hobie's friends would find him in these woods but he had no sooner laid his head down than he drifted off to sleep. His last thoughts were of home and his own folks back there.

His father, Judge Andrew Stearman, would be working in his study, surrounded by law books, writing at his red leather-topped desk with the green shaded lamp at his elbow, perhaps a cigar quietly burning in the ashtray close to hand. Maybe he'd be reading one of his son's letters, which he had diligently written every week detailing his circumstances and health and thoughts on the conflict. They'd have much to discuss when he got home. The judge was a man hungry for information. Knowledge was as meat and drink to him. His aunt Cissy would be in the kitchen seated at the big work-table with Leah and Ginny, the two house girls who helped her with the chores. Small and plump, grey hair neatly braided, she would be shelling peas or sewing, her hands never still, coaxing young Ginny to tell her all the gossip she'd heard in town. Aunt Cis had been widowed for as long as Stearman could remember, had moved in with her brother-in-law and his boy, and run the household ever since. Her son, Harry, took care of the fabric of the judge's large house and the garden. The illness that had killed his father had left Harry a shy, slow, withdrawn young man who was only really happy when he was outdoors, pruning and clipping and tending the grounds.

When Stearman had left for the war, he had been all but engaged to Clare King, arguably the prettiest girl in the county, and at the time, prepared to wait for John to be done with soldiering and come home to marry her. But four years was a long time. She had said she would wait and he couldn't ask for more from her. Her lovely face swam before him as he drifted down into sleep, a perfect oval, sunshine-yellow hair curled and cleverly dressed, green eyes looking at him from under a thick sweep of eyelashes.

'I'm not going anywhere, John,' had been her last words to him.

Stearman sighed in his sleep and murmured her name, but his last thought in fact was to wonder what would become of Bella.

CHAPTER 3

The girl was alone and the carriage was almost empty as the train rocked towards its last stop but one, the town of Randolph. She was young, less than twenty, her watcher figured, a little on the plump side, fair and blue-eyed. She gazed out of the window, her thoughts a million miles away as the pastureland, a hazy purple in the waning evening light, swept past. She wore Sunday best, a navy dress with a neat white collar, fitted at the bodice and full in the skirt, with just a glimpse of a white lace frill on her petticoat at the hem. Only a really close inspection would have shown that the collar was a little frayed, a little yellowed from many washings, and that the skirt bore a neat and barely visible patch. The watcher saw the patch and saw her cheap boots, a little down at heel, and her straw hat, with its little decoration of violets.

She didn't notice the man till he lowered himself on to the seat in front of her, so close their knees were almost touching. She stared at him, then pointedly looked around the carriage, as if to indicate to him that there were plenty other seats, in reality checking to see if there was anyone else in the compartment. She saw no one. He smiled at her and she knew she was in trouble. To her, at nineteen, he seemed pretty old and decrepit, though he was a little above forty, with sallow skin and heavy, dark, greased hair. One cheek had been pitted by smallpox and a powerful smell of blackstrap was on his breath. His clothes were good quality but showing signs of age and wear. For the most part they were black or brown: a black frock-coat over a black vest, darkbrown pants with a thin black stripe, tucked into boots that had not been cleaned in a while.

'No offence, mister, but I'd prefer if you'd go sit somewhere else.'

He didn't speak, just looked at her with an unsettling intensity that made her fidget. She gripped her cloth bag tight on her lap and twisted round to look at the door connecting to the next carriage. The ticket man had been up and down a dozen times, but where was he now?

'Girl travels alone, man knows what she wants,' he said, and his voice frightened her more than anything, but she made a good show of hiding it.

'What I want, sir, is to have you go sit somewhere else.'

'Girls travels alone, man's got a right to think she's lookin' out for a little company.'

'Not this girl,' she said. She tried to rise, to step into the aisle. He blocked her movement with one leg and an arm and shoved her back, then he leaned into her, his face up close.

'You an' me could have a sweet ol' time and no one would ever know.' He grinned at her, with teeth yellowed from tobacco.

'Don't, mister.' She struggled against him, trying to stop him when he reached under her skirt and stroked her calves. His hands were squeezing and sliding up as far as the garter ribbons just below her knees. Her voice became a squeak.

'Let me go, please don't. Please. . . .'

'Don't take on so, girl,' he said patiently, grinning more, a thread of spit connecting his upper and lower lips, his eyes bright with anticipation. 'It'll only be the worse for you if you fight me. Take it easy. I paid the guard to stay away for a while. We won't be disturbed. C'mon. You must've done this a hundred times.' His voice was meant to soothe and reassure but his tone was low and husky and a little breathless; it made her flesh crawl. She redoubled her efforts to cut loose. Inside the carriage, the only sounds were the girl's gasping breaths as she struggled, the scuffing of her boots as she twisted and turned to escape, and the man's loud, heavy breathing. Outside it was almost dark, making a mirror of the window, reflecting so that she could see her attacker hunched over her, like a giant spider, and her own white face. She shut her eyes and twisted away from the foul smell on his breath, praying he wouldn't kill her after it was over.

It took a moment for her to realize that something had changed. His clammy, dirty hands were no longer under her skirts and he had leaned away from her, back into his own seat. She opened her eyes to look and saw that his eyes had widened a little and his grin had become a grimace. The reason was that a small, sharp knife – like the potato knife in the kitchen at home, she thought inconsequentially – was pressed to his neck, just next to the big artery there. She looked up at the person holding the knife, a tall man in a dark coat, his face shadowy because his head was just above the level of the carriage lamps. He held the knife in his left hand. His right hand took a grip on the seated man's collar, forcing him to his feet and then urging him forwards, towards the connecting door. He did no more than tilt his chin to indicate that his prisoner should open the door to allow them to step out on to the platform.

The slipstream of the train was bitterly cold after the comparative warmth of the carriage; the freezing air felt like needles on their exposed skin.

'Winter coming,' the man with the knife said thoughtfully.

'Look. I was just—'

'About to rape a defenceless girl.'

'No,' came the denial. 'Just a bit of fun is all. You and I could go back in there and . . . I mean you could have her first, if you want.'

'Big of you.' The other man nodded. He twisted the knife a little until blood ran on the man's neck. 'But you've got somewhere else you've got to be, haven't you?'

The train had started to slow as it approached a solitary building, just a small shack by the railtracks, an unofficial stop between stations where occasional passengers or parcels were taken aboard. A solitary man, muffled to the eyes against the weather, came out of the shelter of the building carrying a string-tied, brown-paper parcel and pulled himself up into the carriage just behind the engine. The man with the knife hadn't known there was any such place, this solitary shack in the middle of nowhere. A lamp suspended on a projecting bracket was swinging, creaking in the wind. He had never noticed it before; he had intended just to make the creepjump for it. As the train started to pull away with a series of small jerks, he increased the pressure of both the knife on his captive's neck and the hand on his collar, forcing him down the steps and off the train. The man landed awkwardly and almost fell, but righted himself and hurried along beside the train, still arguing his case.

'How am I supposed to get to Randolph tonight? My bag is still in the compartment. Throw it down to me, damn it!'

'You can collect it at the ticket office,' the other man

assured him calmly. 'And while you're there, buy a ticket for another town, because if I see you in Randolph, I'll make sure you get thrown in jail.'

'I won't forget this,' his victim shouted. 'It wasn't supposed. . . .'

His words were lost to the wind as the locomotive picked up speed and rattled round the curving track into the night.

Inside the carriage, the girl, who had been watching out of the window, slowly sat down, turning as the man with the knife came back. He glanced at her, but didn't sit beside her, as she had expected him to do. Stopping just beyond her seat, he looked over his shoulder at her.

'All right?' he asked her gently. She nodded, swallowed hard and tried to smile.

'Thanks.' All right except for the ghostly impression of the man's hands on her body still, his hands inching up to her knees, his intention clear in his face, in his eyes.

The second man nodded, moved further back in the empty compartment and sat down with his back to her. He took something out of his pocket: a letter, she thought, and began to read it. The girl nervously fussed with her hair, tucked away the little trinket on a chain around her neck, putting it back under her collar, and straightened her skirts. Only then did she slowly let all the air out of her lungs and close her eyes with relief.

The girl disembarked at Randolph and lingered on the platform, waiting for the man, to say something more to him. She had put on her coat and a thick muffler and looked slightly dumpy and very young, with her white face and large blue eyes. He picked up the bag he had thrown on to the platform and touched the brim of his hat to her.

'I thought I'd missed you,' she said.

'Wanted to have a word with the guard, after what that

fellow said to you, that he paid him to stay away, but there was no sign of him.'

Over his shoulder she saw the train start to pull out and she watched it for a time before looking back at him. The station wasn't well lit but she could see his face better than before. He had dark-blue eyes and dark hair, was close-shaved, his features stern but good-looking. She guessed he was thirty or thereabouts. His clothes were of good quality; a thick, black, well-cut topcoat, with clean white linen just showing underneath. His boots were well worn but still had the soft sheen of expensive leather.

'I just wanted to thank you. That was a good thing you did.'

'Can I walk you to wherever you're going?' he asked. She hesitated, looked back along the station platform as if expecting someone to be waiting, but there was no one there. She nodded and turned towards the centre of town.

'You kept his bag,' she remarked, and Stearman looked down.

'Nobody at the ticket office this time of night. I'll leave it there in the morning.' *And have a good look through it first,* he thought privately.

'I'm on my way to visit with my cousin, Grace. She works here,' the girl told him as they walked. 'What's your name? Do you live here in Randolph?'

'Yes, ma'am. Name's Stearman, John Stearman. You're just visiting?'

'Yes, sir. I used to live here but I stay in Lydia now. My name's Betsy Ross.' She stopped and made a gesture towards the building on her left. 'This is it.' She smiled.

They had reached the girl's destination, a hotel on the corner of Main Street and Beacon, called Ludlow's, where just about everybody stayed if they were passing through. It had a saloon bar and a restaurant, though it was all small scale and truth be told a little shabby and down at heel.

'It was a pleasure to meet you, Mr Stearman.'

'It was my pleasure, Miss Ross. I hope you have a better journey home.'

He touched the brim of his hat, hoisted his bag on to his shoulder and walked away down Beacon towards the east end of town. The girl watched him for a minute, her face less sunny and animated than it had been in his company; then, when she was sure he was out of sight, she turned and walked back the way she had come.

CHAPTER 4

Stearman climbed the stairs to the third floor of the boarding house, to his room up in the attics. In summer the heat got trapped under the eaves and in winter the wind groaned through the roof beams and whistled through the gaps in the window frames, but it was quiet up here. Mrs Joe had only managed to squeeze two other tenants on to this floor; they were right at the other end of the big, run-down old house and Stearman liked it that way.

Key already in hand, he let himself in, dropped the bag, then turned when he heard a familiar uneven tread on the stair. He stood in the open doorway as a girl came along the long corridor carrying a tray. A small, thin girl, just turned sixteen, she wore her hair in a long thick braid, was clad in clothes that were too short or too tight for her: a faded pink dress and white pinafore, washed to grey. Clumsy, heavy boots on her feet worsened the slight limp she had had since an accident as a child. She smiled at him.

'Hey, Mr Stearman.'

'Hey, Lisbeth.'

'How was your trip?'

'It was OK.'

'I saved you a little supper,' she said, lifting the tray

towards him.

'You'll get in trouble,' he cautioned, but he grinned at her. She grinned back and gave a shrug, for Lisbeth would gladly have broken any number of Mrs Joe's numerous rules, most of them about mealtimes and having callers in the rooms, for Mr Stearman. Lisbeth was an orphan, taken in by Mrs Joe when she was about ten, but not out of the goodness of that lady's heart. She was just Mrs Joe's personal slave, overworked and unpaid.

'Best eat it while it's hot,' she said and turned with a wave to go back downstairs.

Stearman listened till the sound of her uneven tread had died away before taking two steps back into the room. He turned slightly, still holding the tray, to look at the man who had been standing behind the door when he first entered, the man with the gun in his hand and murder in his eyes. The stranger heeled the door shut and cocked the gun.

'How does it feel, mister, somebody aiming a gun at you for a change?' he demanded.

Stearman gazed at him with a look of tired enquiry for a minute, then turned slowly, so as not to excite his visitor. He placed the tray on the table by the window, took off his hat and tossed it on the bed. He had had a pig of a day, he was tired, his back ached, and he hadn't eaten since breakfast. An angry gunman lurking in his room was just about the last straw. An angry, nervous gunman, come to that. Stearman tried for a little humour.

'No offence, but my landlady doesn't like me having callers.'

'You've got ten seconds to tell me why you've been trying to kill me,' the other man warned, shifting his stance a little. Stearman caught the sharp odour of cheap liquor on his breath and a quick glance told him his visitor hadn't slept in a bed, or had a wash, in a week.

'Why would I want to kill you? I don't know you.'

'Shut up! You do know me, damn you. We were both at the ferry, on the Constary, when we hung the Rebel. You were there, don't try to say different.'

The stranger's words hit Stearman like the slap of cold water, jerking him back almost two years to the little clearing in the woods, the smell of smoke from the burning ferry house, the defeated look in the Rebel's eyes and the brutish behaviour of the soldiers, except for the boy Hobie. He stared at the other man, trying to place him there. He had a worn, sunburned face, heavy about the jaw, deep-set blue eyes, big round shoulders, hands like shovels. His clothes were cheap, serviceable, worn and mended many times: farm-hand clothes.

'I was there,' Stearman recalled.

'And now you want a little payback for what we did to you, is that it?'

Stearman thought for a minute about what they had done to him, moved his shoulders in what might have been a shrug, a movement so slight even the stranger didn't notice.

'You hungry?' he asked. The stranger didn't answer. The confrontation he'd planned wasn't going the way it was supposed to. Stearman wasn't cowering in a corner, begging for his life or even putting up a fight of it. He was turning the tray round, lifting aside the tray cloth and offering the plate of beef stew and potatoes, the pot of coffee and the thick hunk of pie. Apple, it looked like. The man's stomach growled traitorously and at that exact moment, he knew he'd got it wrong. He lowered his gun and before he knew what had happened he was sitting at the table, his shoulders slack with defeat.

Stearman poured coffee and prodded the fork into his

big hand.

'How long since you ate?'

'Yesterday I think, maybe Tuesday.'

'I don't recall your name,' Stearman said, though he was pretty sure he had never heard it.

'Randall Anderson. Randy.'

He stared at Stearman as if he might be inclined to argue, then started to eat. Sitting on the other side of the table, Stearman swung his legs up on to the bed and leaned back against the wall, while his uninvited guest made short work of the meat and potatoes and the pie, washing it all down with two cups of coffee from the battered old black coffee pot.

'Looks like that was your first square meal in some time,' Stearman observed.

'Figured it was best to lay low for a while. Then I heard your name mentioned in a bar just down the street there and it just seemed like too much of a coincidence. And besides, I thought you were dead, dead and well and truly buried. Can't blame me for putting two and two together.'

'And coming up with five,' Stearman said drily. 'I've lived here nearly two years. Why would I suddenly decide to come looking for you now? Why did you think it was about the Rebel and the ferry?'

Anderson wiped his hands and mouth on the tray cloth, then turned to stare out of Stearman's only window, which looked out on to Mrs Joe's untidy backyard.

'Because two people from the ferry have already been killed and I know one of them was murdered.'

CHAPTER 5

Randall Anderson's tale was told in a tired monotone, as if he had gone over this story a hundred times in his head and still couldn't make head or tail of it. First, a shot had been fired at him as he made his way home from town one night, about two weeks ago. He worked for two elderly brothers on a smallholding about three miles outside of Lydia, which was the next town along the rail-track heading east. He had a room over the stable, did all the heavy work. After the first shot he hadn't been too bothered, figured it was just youngsters fooling around.

But then there came another shot, on his way into town, early in the morning. This one was no mistake. The bullet plucked at the shoulder seam of his coat, the whine of it so close to his ear that he gave a craven yelp and almost threw himself out of the saddle. His horse made the next decision for him. It took off like a train, ears flat, neck stretched, while Anderson hung on, unable even to look back over his shoulder.

He got good and drunk in town that night while he tried to figure it out. It made no sense to him. He worked hard, kept pretty much to himself, didn't owe any money. Why would anyone want to kill him?

He had to go home eventually though, and for a few days all was well, until the morning he was working in the barn and someone tossed a burning torch through the door, then locked him in. Shocked into immobility for only a few seconds he put the fire out quickly with buckets from a big water butt that was always kept in the barn, then kicked his way out through some loose boards at the back of the building. He half-expected the sniper to be waiting for him when he rounded the building, but there was no one in sight.

The Windom brothers, his employers, were not at all happy with him. They had been grudgingly tolerant of what they thought was a three-day bender in town, when he had in fact been too scared to come home, but the fire in the barn was a whole other thing. Admittedly it hadn't burned down and the damage was minimal, but they felt they could no longer rely on him and so they told him to pack his gear and go. Casual labour was cheap and easy to come by since the war. Anderson shed no tears for his loss. He made a bundle of the little he had, saddled up, rode to Randolph and got himself lost in the rabbit warren of shacks and tents they called Canvas Town, on the south side of the rail-tracks.

'I broke cover and come into town yesterday. That's when I heard your name mentioned.'

'What did you hear?' Stearman asked.

'Fella said his sister's baby girl died and he wanted to help with the funeral, she was so cut up about it. The other man said you had made a nice coffin for a friend of his who lost a child. I remembered your name. Stearman. I butted in and asked where I could find you. That's when I got it in my head that it must be about the ferry. Was all I could think of.'

'You said two others had died. What happened to them?'

'Phil Hunter, one of us at the ferry, died a month ago. He was on his own, just working his patch, him and his old mule, when he dropped down dead. Doctor said it was his heart give out. He'd been pretty sick with his lungs for a while. His sister sent me word so I went along to the funeral and when I was there I was told that Nolan Rawl had been killed on his way home after a poker game. He was back-shot for sixteen lousy dollars. I'm still friends with his brother Luther. They were like twins; maybe you noticed.'

Stearman shook his head. He remembered vaguely the pale, poorly-looking man and two others with fair hair. He supposed they had been the Rawl brothers.

'The thing is, two are dead and someone's been after me. All of us were at the ferry together.'

Stearman didn't think the evidence was that strong for a conspiracy against Anderson but he kept his own counsel.

'Do you know the situation of any others?' he asked.

'You remember Sergeant Parry?'

'Yes. He hit the boy, Hobie.'

'I heard he lives here in Randolph. He's a councilman, calls himself Major Parry. Must've gone off to find another war to fight to get that promotion,' Anderson said scornfully. But with that revelation, Stearman wondered if he hadn't pointed out a good motive for removing any witnesses of what happened that day.

'What about the boy?'

'Hobie? I don't know about him. He was on his way home when he fell in with us. Said he lived in a little place called Dansing with his folks.'

· 'And the other man. The man who hit me?'

'Colonel Bell. I don't know about him either. We all split up a week after the ferry. The only people I've seen are Phil and Luther.'

Stearman swung his legs down to the floor and stood up. It was late and he was bone weary, but he had a feeling he wasn't going to lose his new house guest in a hurry.

'Why don't you bunk down here tonight? I think that would be better than trying to get across town this late. You can decide what to do in the morning.'

'Thanks. I appreciate that, and thanks for the supper. You've been real decent about everything. But tomorrow I'm going to try to get to Luther and warn him and then maybe I'll try to find Hobie. That's what I'm going to do.'

At two in the morning, Stearman was still awake, his head pillowed on his arm, staring at the stain that looked like a crouching cat on the ceiling, where the rain had got in. Anderson was asleep in the opposite corner, wrapped in Stearman's comforter. He had lain down facing into the room but when sleep claimed him he had rolled on to his natural position, on his back, and was gently snoring. Stearman, listening to him and the fitful night-time sounds of the old house, which was never completely quiet, found himself examining his reasons for helping Randall Anderson. He and the others at the ferry had done some pretty bad things in the last weeks of the war: hanging crimes, had they been caught, and they had tried to kill him that day with no more thought than if they had drawn a bead on a rabbit. If someone was hunting him then in all likelihood he deserved what was coming to him.

After Hobie left him he had walked for a day and a half before reaching a farm where the people took care of him till he felt well enough to travel, for he was concussed from the blow to his head and ill for nigh on a week. Then he was taken by the farmer's eldest son in the farm cart to the nearest village. From there he negotiated a series of rides from one hamlet to another until he finally reached the railroad and completed his journey in comparative comfort.

But because of his temporary infirmity and having lost Bella, it took him at least three weeks longer to reach home than it should have done. In that time he lost almost his entire family.

Diphtheria had cut a swath through his hometown like a medieval plague. When it slipped away, as quietly as it had come, almost half the townspeople were dead, young and old, rich and poor alike, including his father, Judge Andrew Stearman, his sister-in-law and all but two of the judge's household. Ginny Parker, who had served the Stearman family in one capacity or another for thirty years, and Harry Stearman, his cousin, both survived. They did all they could for the sick and buried them when they died; it fell to them to explain to the newly returned Major Stearman what had happened.

He had come home so hopefully, expecting to slip back into the comfortable, loving circle of his family, expecting to be nurtured and cared for and to have some of the invisible wounds of the war he had been away fighting soothed and healed by his father and aunt and Ginny and the others. But there was only Harry, who seemed to have aged a dozen years with what he had seen and done in the last weeks, and Ginny, who had grown gaunt with overwork.

Stearman did what he had been doing for the last four years and took charge, quietly, efficiently, easing the burden from Harry and managing to find some help for Ginny. There were plenty of orphans in the town in need of work and a home, truth to tell. Harry returned to what he did best: the garden, the stable, and those household chores that the women couldn't manage.

There was only one other thing he needed to know and it was Ginny, scarcely able to endure giving him more bad news, who told him, sitting at the kitchen table three nights after his return, that Clare King was gone too. But not to the bone yard. No, Clare was very much alive. She had met a man from New York, three months since, and had left town with him. They had married a few weeks later. Kyle Shepherd had sold boots and other leather goods to the army and had made a fortune out of it. In his favour it had to be said they were good boots, not the shoddy things that had disintegrated after a month and which had been the heartbreak of many a Union soldier.

'She gave me a letter to give you,' Ginny said as she fetched the envelope from its place on one of the kitchen shelves, where it had been propped for three months. Stearman took it, looked at the familiar schoolgirl slope and blinked at it before taking out the single slip of folded blue paper. He read that she was tired waiting for him, unsure of how she felt about him after all, but quite sure that life in New York with the wealthy Mr Shepherd would suit her better than life in a rural backwater with a man with little or no ambition, and nothing more to show for four years of war than the rank of major. She closed by saying she wished him well and hoped he and his family wouldn't think too badly of her.

Looking up at Ginny, Stearman realized that she knew what was in the letter. In fact she had steamed it open the day it arrived. She already knew Clare had eloped with Shepherd, so she had a rough idea what it said. She had shown it to Aunt Cis, who, far from being shocked at a servant taking such an action, agreed that she had done it for the best and resolved not to tell John until he was home.

'I'd say you had a narrow escape,' Ginny told him, but her eyes looked at him with concern. He suddenly looked drained of life and hope. He put the letter in his shirt pocket and got up to find his father's best brandy. He poured some

37

for himself and Ginny and for Harry, who had come in to see how Stearman had taken the news, and began to drink, steadily and relentlessly till the bottle lay tilted and empty on the table and he was unconscious with his head on his arms. Harry carried him to bed and took off his boots and pants and pulled the quilt over him. Then he sat in a chair and watched over him all night, only slipping away in the morning when Stearman woke up with a thick head and sour stomach, and a resolve not to drown his sorrows again.

He hadn't kept to that resolve. He had got good and drunk often since then, but the length of time between drinking jags had grown longer so that now he couldn't remember when he had last brought home a bottle from Wheatley's store.

He had endured life in his old home for a few months but finally admitted to himself that he could stand it no longer. The reminders and mementoes of happier times were everywhere. There was no escape from the past in this rambling old house. He asked Harry and Ginny to take care of the place for him, set it up with the bank so that they would get an allowance every month to take care of things and pay wages. His mother had been a wealthy woman and his father had been careful. There was money to spare and Harry particularly needed stability and the familiarity of the only home he had ever known.

They tried to make him stay but he told them it was just for a little while. The war had made him restless, he told them. He just wanted to travel a little. So he packed a single bag and left, promising to write, which he did. Every week without fail he wrote to both of them, telling them where he was, what he was doing and whom he had met, none of which bore any resemblance to the reality of the life he had chosen for himself. He walked everywhere or rode the trains, took low-paid jobs where he could find them, worked hard and tried to bury himself in meaningless physical labour, withholding all but his name from anybody who tried to get close. He cleaned stables, drove freight wagons, cut trees, dug ditches and mended fences. He endured all kinds of weather and hardship and made few friends. That was how he wanted it. For a while the vagabond life suited him.

Then one day he found himself in Randolph, having been hired to deliver a load of timber, some of which was destined for the workshop behind the Elmhirst Funeral Parlour owned by Harry Barclay. There he met the man who made the coffins, Gunter Brand. He was a small man, wrinkled like an old apple, with half-moon glasses and receding hairline, dapper when he wasn't working, focused and silent when he was. He had injured his hand with a saw when Stearman met him; seeing his difficulty, Stearman had offered to saw the lumber for him, did one or two other jobs and ended up staying on. He was poorly paid but was drawn to Gunter's carpentry skills and found himself wanting to learn from him. The older man had taught him as much as he could but had been surprised and generously pleased when his pupil had effortlessly outstripped him.

'You'll do,' he told him. 'You've got a natural feel for the wood.'

With cholera decimating Canvas Town it took the two of them to keep up with demand, but Stearman wasn't his father's son for nothing. When he saw that Barclay was prepared to pay him only half the going rate as long as he could get away with it, despite the fact that he was now doing the lion's share of the work, he thanked Gunter for all his help and advice and walked out of the workshop. Harry Barclay turned up at his rooming house an hour later to offer him full pay. He had had good relations with the undertaker ever since and word had got around that John Stearman was nobody's fool.

Gunter had died six months later. He had stayed late one night to put the finishing touches on a special casket for some rich body from Brewer Street and was found in the morning, sitting in the chair by the stove, both of them cold and dead. The doctor pronounced a heart attack. Stearman made him the best coffin he was capable of constructing and helped carry him to his grave. Gunter had left all his tools, fifty dollars on deposit at the bank and a trunk of old clothes and personal effects to Stearman. Stearman had gone through the trunk half-heartedly later that day, but then he closed it up, pushed it into a corner of the workshop and forgot about it.

He worked alone at the workshop after that, going through the motions, enjoying the carpentry but not the coffin-making. He had already begun to think of moving on when Randall Anderson had come to call.

If he had not left Bella by the river that day and gone into the woods to see what was going on, he would have arrived home at the same time as the diphtheria epidemic and would most likely have died along with the others, or at the least would have had to endure their suffering and watch them die.

That was something to be thankful for, he supposed, as he turned tiredly on to his side to try to sleep. Wasn't it?

CHAPTER 6

Stearman had come alone, riding on a borrowed mount into the dense woodland the locals called Hutton's Woods. All around him the leaves wore autumn dress, bronze and yellow and red, some still green. The winding path was strewn with with dry foliage. He could hear the sound of running water close by and some muted birdsong. Otherwise all was quiet.

Luther Rawl lived here, four miles east of town. According to Randall Anderson he collected and sold wood for a living, mostly gathering deadfall or felling damaged trees, trimming and cutting it to sell, generally to the residents of Canvas Town. He kept a few hogs, attended a regular Friday-night poker game with one or two friends, Randall Anderson amongst them; he even went to prayer meetings on Sundays.

Stearman had left Anderson behind, stashing him in the empty room at the other end of the corridor with a share of Stearman's breakfast and a warning not to move around too much till he got back. Anderson had stared at him like a big old stray dog, shaggy and none too bright. He had sunk down on to the bed in the otherwise empty room, with his big hands splayed on his knees. His expression was one of

41

dumb surprise and wonder at finding himself in this situation.

Stearman had been wondering about the same thing as he rode into the clearing where Hunter's cabin was sited. What in the world was he doing here? He looked around the untidy yard, at the small, rough cabin, the woodshed and the hog-pen off to one side. He dismounted and tethered the horse near the edge of the clearing, then walked up to the cabin door. His carpenter's eye noted the rough construction of the building; most of it was axe-cut, the wood undressed, unpainted, turning grey, curling like dried paper with age and weather. This cabin had been here a long time, longer than the town, long before the railroad. It also looked as if it had never enjoyed a woman's presence. The two front-facing windows were filthy and uncurtained and the porch was cluttered with dirty boots and work tools.

Stearman knocked and waited. After a minute he knocked again but almost at once turned away and started to walk round to the back of the cabin, for he was sure he had heard a sound, man-made, wood knocking on wood. The backyard was as untidy and cluttered as the front, with piles of fresh-cut lumber stacked under a lean-to and loose branches and wood shavings lying all around a big tree stump, into which an axe was embedded. But there was no one in sight.

'Anybody home? Mr Rawl?' Stearman called out.

The autumn sun suddenly went behind a cloud and a cold easterly breeze stirred the trees, making the dry leaves rustle and sigh overhead; Stearman felt the grip of unease at the back of his neck.

He returned to the front of the building. This time he tried the handle of the cabin door, a simple wooden latch that admitted him to the cabin's interior. It was basically just one room divided by a curtain strung across the breadth of the room to separate the sleeping area, which had an unmade bed, a chair and a shelf on which stood a candle and some books. In the main area there was a table and two chairs; an old leather armchair was set beside a wood-burning stove. More shelves carried some books and some folded clothing; the remains of a meal were still on the table: greasy bacon rind and cornbread. There was no sign of any-thing amiss in here, at least.

He went back to the porch and headed for the woodshed, a building almost as long as the house but with a low, shake roof, a single window and no chimney breast. The door was held open with a sledgehammer, standing head down. Cautiously he looked in then stepped into the gloom. The place was rich with the familiar smells of wood shavings, resin and linseed oil. Uncut wood was stacked along the back wall, a workbench stood under the window wall, lit-tered with tools, and standing against the far wall was Luther Rawl.

Stearman remembered him right away, the blunt nose, the big jaw and blond hair and the little scar under his eye. His frayed and elderly brown coat was too long in the arms and his pants too tight across the thighs. Moreover he was afraid: fear was in his eyes, fear was making the cords in his neck stand out.

'What do you want?' he demanded. He was holding an axe in one hand, a short-handled implement with a wicked-looking blade, but he didn't appear to have any other weapon.

'Randall Anderson asked me to give you a message.'

Rawl swallowed noisily, his eyes flickering over Stearman, past him to the door and then back again.

'What message?'

43

'Said to tell you somebody's after him, maybe the same person that killed your brother. He thought it might be connected with the ferry. You remember what happened at the ferry, on the Constarry River?'

'I remember. And I remember you. You were the one tried to stop us. Seems to me you're the one most like to bring me trouble.'

'No, sir, I'm not your trouble,' Stearman said quietly, taking a half-step as if to turn away, but then he stopped and swung back.

'Something's already happened, hasn't it?'

'Might be something, might be nothing.' Luther shrugged. Stearman waited, with no more than a look of mild enquiry on his face. 'Somebody took a shot at me the other day on the way home from town. Then on Saturday, I was working in here, I had a few drinks and fell asleep and when I woke up . . .' He stopped and turned to look out of the window, his Adam's apple working. 'When I woke, I found somebody had killed my hogs. Cut their throats. I thought it might have been. . . .' He didn't finish, didn't share with Stearman what he thought it might have been.

'What did you do?'

'Do?' Rawl seemed baffled by the question.

'Did you report it to the sheriff?'

'Hell no. Might as well report it to one of my dead hogs. What happened to Randy?'

'Just about the same as you, except they tried to burn him alive in a barn.'

Luther grunted something that Stearman couldn't make out. Then suddenly his eyes widened, he grimaced and his body stiffened. Something glinted in the middle of his chest and a dark stain began to spread out from it, blossoming across his buttoned-up coat: a dark, deep crimson.

Stearman stared, his brain at first unable to make any sense of what he was seeing. Instinctively, he dropped down to a crouch and twisted round to see if there was someone in the doorway behind him. His first thought was that Rawl had been stabbed, that a knife had been thrown from the doorway, but as he got closer, still in a defensive crouch, he saw that the blade in the middle of Luther's chest had entered his body from behind, from a thrust through a gap in the wooden wall boards, into his back. The blade was all that was holding him up.

Just as Stearman reached him, he started to slump forward, his body sliding free of the blade and dropping face down on to the earthen floor. The blood was pumping out of his chest now, an unstoppable fountain of lifeblood, with a hot, metallic smell. Stearman turned him over, raising his head slightly. His face was grey, his eyes already beginning to dull over as death approached and his breath came in short, jerking gasps.

'It's bad, isn't it?' he gasped. He continued to fight for breath for several minutes more before he died, his disbelieving stare fixed on Stearman. Stearman pressed his eyelids down and sat back on his haunches, shocked by the speed of it all. Barely two or three minutes had passed since he had walked in the door and yet Luther Rawl was dead, and maybe the man who had killed him was still outside.

He stood and hurried to the door. He paused just long enough to take a quick look outside to make sure there was no one waiting for him on the other side, then ran round to the side of the woodshed where the knife had come through. It was still stuck in the wall, a long, tapering butcher's knife. The killer had stood here, listening, maybe planning to kill Luther with the knife when he emerged from the woodshed, but then he had seen another opportunity: a gap in the planking, at chest height, and Luther had been standing close enough for the blade to reach him.

Stearman pulled the knife clear to get a better look. Then he heard a sound to his left, the snap of a twig under foot, and he turned and ran towards the sound, into the trees behind the building. He caught a glimpse of black clothing, saw a glint of something metallic and then his prey was gone deeper into the woods, running hard and veering to the left. Stearman followed, ducking beneath low branches, vaulting over dead ones, just about keeping up with the running man ahead of him. At one point, the figure in the distance seemed to hesitate for a second about whether to turn right or left. Stearman threw the knife which he was still holding, but heard the thud as it struck a tree trunk. His target turned right and disappeared into the thicket. Stearman followed doggedly. He altered tack, taking a diagonal route that he gauged would bring him out slightly ahead of the running man, but when he broke out of the thicket, his quarry was gone. He had come full circle and had reached the track that led up to the cabin.

He bent over with his hands on his knees, winded and angry with himself for not having gone round to the back of the woodshed sooner. His breathing slowed and he tried to listen for the other man. At first there were only the sounds of the woodland: the dry rustle of leaves and that faraway sound of running water. But above that came another sound that he couldn't make out at first. He started back to the cabin and the sound grew louder, more distinct, a crackling and snapping, and with it, the smell of woodsmoke. He reached the little clearing where the cabin stood and groaned at what he saw.

The woodshed was ablaze. Already, in just a few minutes,

the building had become a fireball of flame and heat; black billows of smoke curled upwards from the inferno. Stearman worriedly watched the direction of the smoke. There had been a breeze earlier but it had dropped now, so he thought the cabin and the woods were probably safe from the fire. He watched from a distance, standing beside his nervous mount, murmuring quietly and stroking her chest to calm her. She was leery of the fire.

He recalled finding himself in a similar situation during the war, when he and a small scouting party had been hunted by Confederate soldiers through dense woodland just like the nearby thicket. The Rebels had outnumbered Stearman's men four to one, but he had split his men into three groups, one group to act as decoys, while the other two sheered off to the right and left, then doubled back, encircling the enemy. The Rebels, tricked and then trapped, had fought back with cold fury, refusing the chance to surrender that was offered to them, and a skirmish had turned into a bloody rout. The Unionists hadn't taken many prisoners. Stearman had received a commendation and his promotion to major for that day's bloody work.

But this time he was the one who had been led by the nose, taken around in an ever-decreasing circle of futility, while his adversary doubled back on him and put torch to the property. He had been soundly outflanked by a clever and dangerous killer. Now he knew how those Rebels had felt.

He watched the fire until it had burnt down to almost nothing and the woodshed, being constructed entirely of timber and having so much combustible material inside, was nothing but hot, smoking ash.

When it was cool enough to approach, he picked over the embers until he found what was left of Luther: charred flesh and bones, a belt buckle and, to one side of him, the head of the axe he had been holding, still bright and sharp amongst the embers.

Stearman returned to his horse and mounted up, turning for home through the leafy woodland. When he glanced back a mile or so later, there was hardly any trace in the sky of the fierce fire that had burned a short while ago, only a faint wisp of smoke. He settled back in the saddle, turning to face front again. Now that the danger seemed to be over, now that he had time to reflect, he fell to wondering. Why had the killer in the woods spared him?

CHAPTER 7

At supper, Stearman begged an extra plate of fried pork belly and cabbage from Lisbeth, on the pretext that he had not eaten anything at midday. She heaped his plate, pleased to be able to give him something back for all the little kindnesses he did for her. She watched as he took an extra slice of bread, poured himself more coffee and carried the meal off to his room, saying over his shoulder that he would bring the dishes back later.

Lisbeth was lame in her leg but not in her head. She knew there was someone else moving around in the empty room at the end of the corridor. She had heard him moving around during the day when the house was quiet, had heard him cough once. Mr Stearman was hiding somebody up there, for what reason she couldn't begin to guess, but she wouldn't dream of giving him away, not for the world.

Mrs Joe had arrived in the kitchen. She was short and stout, with a wiry frizz of grey hair that, like her voice, could scour, and she had the eyes of a professional card-sharp. She had an unpleasant disposition at the best of times, but today her corns were hurting and Lisbeth was an easy target for her foul temper. She struck the girl a ringing blow to the head and then gave her a one-handed shove towards the kitchen sink.

'What you gawping at, girl? Haven't you got any work to do, standing around staring at nothing? Git on before I show you what for, lazy, worthless no-account.'

Lisbeth, used to her employer's ill-treatment, ducked her head and began clattering dishes into the hot water she had poured from the kettle a minute ago, but she smiled a secret smile: she knew something Mrs Joe didn't.

Randall Anderson was relieved to see Stearman, especially since he had brought food. He fell on it like a starving wolf, seated at the table by the window, this room being an exact replica of Stearman's room down the corridor. Only when he had mopped the last drop of gravy with the last corner of bread and taken a couple of swallows of coffee did he raise his head to look enquiringly at Stearman, who was seated opposite him, waiting for him to finish.

'How'd it go?' he asked, and he knew by Stearman's expression that it hadn't gone well.

'I'm sorry but Luther's dead.' The unsparing words seemed to deflate Anderson. He slumped back in his chair, looking suddenly tired and defeated.

'What happened?' he asked. Stearman told him, as briefly and matter-of-factly as possible, while Anderson stared out of the tiny window at the alley behind the rooming house.

'You want my opinion?' Stearman asked him and Anderson nodded. 'Make yourself scarce. Put a couple of states between you and this man, whoever he is.'

'I've got some relatives in West Virginia,' Anderson said hopefully, groping for something to hold on to, starting to make a plan that allowed him to stay alive a little while longer.

'Maybe you ought to take the train. You could put a deal of miles behind you in no time,' Anderson nodded, looking even more like a shaggy old dog, badly in need of a bath.

'You've been real decent, Stearman, more than I deserve, all things considered. You know, nothing went right for any of us after the ferry, not for me, or Luther, Nolan or Phil Hunter, we just couldn't make anything of our lives. My pa would've said it was a judgement on us.'

This ungainly bear of a man, slow but not stupid, had taken a wrong turn at the tail end of the war but somehow, with dogged determination, had woven a new life for himself out of the rags of the old one, had become hard-working, steady and more tolerant. He seemed baffled that, despite all his efforts, he had come to this, hunted and friendless, except for Stearman: the last man he had expected to help.

'You went a little crazy back then. But you tried to turn it around.'

'Yeah, don't get me wrong, I'm no angel, but I've tried to be straight in my dealings since then.'

'So, first thing in the morning we'll go to the station, put you on an eastbound. How are you fixed for money?'

'I'm all right that way, thanks, if you were offering.'

'I was. We'll get you on your way and when you're fixed, you can write me a line or two, let me know how you go on.'

'Sounds as good a plan as any, I guess,' Anderson said, and he stood up to shake Stearman's hand with a crushing grip.

'I'll see you in the morning,' Stearman lifted the dirty dishes and left him in the dingy little room. He returned the crockery to the kitchen, where Lisbeth was washing a mountain of supper things. She turned around as he came in and smiled at him.

'You look like you've got your work cut out for you,' he remarked, and she rolled her eyes.

'I sure ain't fond of supper-time,' she conceded, but with her ever-present cheerfulness.

'No one to help you?' he asked. She shook her head. He lifted the dishrag from the rail on the front of the stove and began to dry the dishes for her. She stared for a minute, but didn't make more than a token protest and between them they soon had the supper dishes done, dried and stacked away. Wearily, she poured two cups of coffee and sat down at the table with him to drink it.

'Does your leg hurt sometimes?' Stearman asked when he saw her grimace and shift her position slightly.

'Just when I've had a busy day. It's fine when I'm rested.'

'And when would that be? Midnight? She doesn't cut you much slack, does she?' he said with a nod of the head towards the private back parlour where Mrs Joe more or less lived.

'She took me in, gave me a place to sleep and food to eat. I try to remember that,' Lisbeth said dutifully, more than a little afraid of being overheard.

'Sure. She just doesn't know President Lincoln abolished slavery,' Stearman observed, and Lisbeth allowed him a low chuckle. Then she leaned forward, conspiratorially, lowering her voice to ask him, 'Did your friend in the empty room enjoy his supper?'

Stearman blinked, then smiled and shook his head.

'I could have used a spy like you at Bull Run,' he said.

'I won't tell anyone, cross my heart, Mr Stearman,' she promised, matching her words with the age-old action of passing two fingers quickly over her chest.

'I know, sweetheart. He's an old war buddy of mine, down on his luck. He's leaving first thing.'

'I'll make sure you get extra bacon.' She grinned.

CHAPTER 8

Stearman never knew what woke him, some alteration in the workings of the old house, some slight change to the creaking and settling of cooling timber and tired people.

He rose and dressed quickly and quietly in all but his boots and unlocked the door to look outside. The corridor was black dark and Stearman waited to let his eyes adjust before moving as stealthily as he could towards Anderson's door at the far end. As he approached it he could see that the door was slightly ajar; just an inch, no more, but that was all wrong.

He stood silently outside the door for some minutes, listening intently for any sound at all that would tell him what was going on inside. At first all seemed quiet, then there came a soft moan. He pushed the door wide open and stepped quickly inside. He was aware of two things right off. First that Randall Anderson was lying on the floor beside the bed and second, that there was someone else in the room, behind the door, coming at Stearman with a raised arm.

He blocked the blow that was coming at him with his elbow and at the same time drove his own right fist into the body of his attacker, making good contact with his ribs. The intruder gave a grunt of pain but at the same time threw himself against Stearman and grappled with him. In the

53

tussle, both men stumbled into the corridor, where Stearman found himself wedged against the wall with a hand around his throat. He groped for the other man's face, jamming a thumb into one eye, then rammed his own heel down on to the other's instep. The man gave a yelp of pain and tore himself free of Stearman. He threw a last wild punch that connected with the wall instead of Stearman's head, then turned, bolted down the corridor, and leapt down the stairs three at a time.

Stearman returned to the room and knelt down to have a look at Anderson. He had pulled himself into a half-sitting position, leaning against the side of the bed, holding both hands to his belly. Stearman lit the lamp on the bedside table and brought it closer to have a look.

Anderson's pupils were wide with shock, two dark circles in an ashen face. A cut on his scalp was bleeding but not heavily, and his lower lip was also cut, but his worst injury was under his two cupped hands. Stearman gently prised them open to look, peeling aside the shirt that Anderson had gone to bed wearing. The wound looked like nothing at all, just a nick, less than an inch across, but it was deep and it had punctured something inside. He was haemorrhaging, had already lost too much blood. It had pooled in his lap and gathered in a black puddle underneath him.

'Is she gone?' Anderson asked weakly.

'He's gone,' Stearman said, trying not to show his distress at Anderson's condition.

'Did he hurt you?'

'No. But I think I put one of his eyes out.'

Randy nodded, tried to smile but grimaced with the effort, then was quiet for a bit, concentrating on his breathing. 'Did you see who it was?' he asked.

'It was too dark.' But there had been something familiar

about him. Stearman tried to remember what it was, something he had encountered recently. 'I'm going to get a doctor for you, Randy. I won't be long. Try to hold on.'

'Don't go yet,' Anderson begged, gripping Stearman's forearm. 'Try to find Hobie, will you? Tell him he's in danger. He was a decent kid. He didn't want any part of what we did.'

'Don't worry about it. Save your strength.'

Anderson's breathing had become laboured, his colour more grey than white. He was staring at the half-open door, his eyes wide with fear, but it was only Lisbeth, in her nightgown, holding a lamp.

'It's all right, Randy. This is just Lisbeth. She cooked your supper tonight.'

The girl knelt down, putting her lamp on the floor nearby. She peered down at the wound and then looked for confirmation at Stearman. He was surprised by how calm she was and how practical. She fetched the towel from the washstand, folded it over and pressed it against the wound, where it almost instantly became crimson.

'You'll be all right. Mr Stearman will get Doc Harmon and—'

'No, don't go, don't leave me. Don't leave me.' Anderson gripped the girl's hand and increased his grip on Stearman. 'Guess I . . . guess I won't be taking that . . . train . . . after all.' He drew a breath that seemed to hurt him terribly, held on to it a long time, then let it trickle out.

He slipped away right after that, on a little sigh, his head sinking forward, making him seem as if he was gazing down at the fatal wound. They laid him down on the floor and Lizbeth pulled the bedcover over him, drawing it almost reluctantly up over his face after Stearman closed his eyes.

'Was it the man on the stairs that killed him, Mr

Stearman?' she asked, keeping her voice to a respectful whisper.'

'You saw somebody on the stairs?'

'Yes, sir. He almost knocked me down.'

'Did you recognize him?'

'No,' she said, all at once sounding tired; her thin face looked pale and suddenly very young. 'You see, I hadn't gotten my lamp lit then. I just saw that he had on a black coat and had dark hair.'

'I think we ought to be geting you back to bed,' Stearman observed gently. She nodded, but suddenly foresaw all kinds of delays and problems.

'What about Mrs Joe? Shouldn't we get the sheriff?' Then, soft and pityingly, 'Did he have any kinfolk?'

Stearman helped her to her feet, put her lamp back in her hand and steered her towards the door.

'Don't worry about it. I'll take care of everything, and no, he didn't have any kin.'

Lisbeth paused to look back over her shoulder at the dead man on the floor.

'He seemed like a nice man,' she murmured.

'No,' Stearman said, not sparing her illusions, 'he wasn't a nice man. But he was trying to be a better one.' He put a hand on her shoulder and walked out of the room with her. He was about to tell her again to go to bed when they both heard the sound of approaching footsteps and a voice like a rasp, demanding to know what was going on in her respectable house at this ungodly hour of the night, and what was Lisbeth doing up here in her nightgown?

CHAPTER 9

Because she knew Mrs Joe better than anybody, Lisbeth saw that Stearman couldn't explain any of this without her help. She stepped right in and told Mrs Joe that Randall Anderson had come looking for a room late, when Mrs Joe was already abed. He had asked for supper, she elaborated, but Lisbeth had said it was too late and showed him to the attic room. Later on she had gone to investigate the noise upstairs and met the killer as he fled from the house. She said she had found Mr Anderson dying on the floor and that was when Mr Stearman had arrived.

Stearman meekly held his peace, realizing for himself the difficulty of explaining Anderson's presence in the attic room, though he saw that his unpleasant landlady was casting about for someone to blame in all of this. Her eye was tending to fall on Lisbeth. There was nothing for it but to send for the sheriff. When he arrived, Lisbeth and Stearman repeated their story for his benefit.

Sheriff Moss appeared to be entirely too old to be a lawman. He looked about a hundred. He was thinner than a spoon and looked almost frail, and had papery skin. His white hair was close cropped and he sported a small, neatly clipped moustache. He moved slow and spoke little, had an old-fashioned courtesy to him that sat well with the neat black suit and clean but slightly frayed shirts that he wore. But Stearman wasn't taken in. He had been raised by a man just like him, who hid a razor-sharp legal mind behind a rumpled, absent-minded presence and who fooled everybody with his small-town geniality.

Sheriff Moss, known to everyone as Doc, had tamed the town ten years ago and kept it that way, with the help of two good deputies and the town council on his side, mostly. He didn't allow guns to be worn on the streets and he had no favourites when it came to arresting drunks and law-breakers. He liked to nip trouble in the bud, which made for an easier life all round. If he hadn't had Canvas Town to take care of, his life would have been tolerable.

He begged a cup of coffee from Lisbeth and complimented her on the sweet biscuits she served with it. He knew Lisbeth did every bit of work in this house and that Mrs Joe held the threat of homelessness and destitution over the child's head to keep it that way. He didn't like Dora Forbes, known to all as Mrs Joe after her husband died and left her the rooming-house, but she ran a respectable establishment and had never had any trouble, though the rooming-house was about as far down the heap as it was possible to go without living in a tent. She wasn't going to lose any clientele over this business, except maybe for the residents who might think they were going to get the blame.

They were sitting in Mrs Joe's kitchen, which was painted a depressing shade of dark green and always reminded Stearman of the mortuary in the Elmhirst Funeral Home. They sat around the big central worktable, which though elderly and battle-scarred, was spotlessly clean thanks to Lisbeth.

'I was wondering how easy it would have been for an intruder to get in, Mrs Forbes,' he remarked to Mrs Joe, in a casual manner that shouldn't have got her back up but it did. 'Is the outer door kept locked?'

'Yes it is,' she responded sharply. 'All my tenants got keys to the front door and to their own rooms. Some of them work late or in shifts. Wouldn't do to have them waking the whole house at all hours to get in.'

Besides which, any five-year-old could open the front door by the simple means of lifting the handle slightly, which freed the door entirely from the lock. The sheriff had already observed this.

'Well, that's very clear, thank you. Now perhaps we might excuse these two ladies, Mr Stearman, while you and I have a word. It's pretty late and I think I have all the information from them I need for now.'

Mrs Joe said, 'Tut,' and bustled out of the room with a very tired and worried-looking Lisbeth right behind her, in a nightgown that was too thin for the autumn and too old to be anything but a dishrag. Lisbeth paused at the door to look back at Stearman; he gave her a wink and mouthed that he'd be OK.

'How's the coffin-making business, John?' the sheriff asked when they were quite alone. 'You still work for Harry Barclay at Elmhirst?'

'Yes, sir.'

'Expect you'll have the measuring-up of me one of these days.'

'I just got back from a buying trip. Bought some fine mahogany and one or two good pieces of oak.'

'Oh, plain pine will do for me, son. Town don't pay me enough for mahogany. Now,' he went on, turning slightly in his chair to get a better look at Stearman, 'suppose you tell me what really happened tonight.'

Ever since he had stepped into his bedroom to find Randall Anderson behind the door waiting for him, Stearman's life had been a tangle of lies and complications. But Anderson's death had moved matters beyond his competence, so he sighed, rubbed his face and the back of his neck to wake himself up a little. Then he began to tell the sheriff the long and involved story that began at the ferry on the Constary River and ended this night with a dead man in Mrs Joe's attic room.

He didn't tell Doc Moss that he had been there when the knife went into Luther Rawl's back, only that he had found him already dead and that he had intended to call at the sheriff's office this morning to tell him what had happened but he had got back late and, frankly, hadn't wanted to miss his supper. The sheriff was very interested, however, in the names of two of the three remaining participants of the events in the ferry.

'So Major Parry was there, you say?'

'He was just Sergeant Parry then. As a matter of fact Randall Anderson was curious as to where his promotion came from, since the fighting was over.'

'I always knew he was full of piss and vinegar,' Doc Moss observed with satisfaction. 'And this other man was a colonel? Bell, did you say? I heard tell of a Quartus Bell one time.'

'I never knew his first name.'

'He was a hellfire preacher before the war. How he got to be "colonel" I don't know but he was known for having a mean streak towards his own men and last I heard he got drummed out, after he got half his platoon killed.'

'Could be the same man.'

'Well.' Doc Moss paused to press a thumb to his moustache,

smoothing it thoughtfully. 'And what about this other fellow, Hobie?'

'Randall asked me to find him, warn him he might be in danger. They were his last words. But I'm not convinced there's a connection to all this and the ferry. Between them they committed a fair amount of mayhem in the last months of the war. Could be anybody on their trail.'

'Or maybe one of the remaining three. Or even you,' Doc said, and Stearman lifted one shoulder and smiled.

'Sheriff, that would make me just about the stupidest murderer who ever lived.'

'No,' Doc said with a little nod, 'I already hung him.'

'Well, I certainly wouldn't want to kill Hobie. Boy saved my life.'

'Let's just hope that Luther's and Randall's deaths were caused by some other, separate feud and that it ended here, tonight. Easier for me to look into, easier all round.'

The sheriff got to his feet, reached for his battered, flat-brimmed hat and patted his pockets for no apparent reason.

'See m'self out,' he said with a nod. 'I'll send some deputies over in the morning for the body.'

Stearman turned out the lamp above the table and headed for his bed. Lisbeth was perched on the stairs, waiting for him, her nightgown tucked under her feet for warmth.

'What did the sheriff say? Is everything all right?'

' 'Course it is. He thinks you were very brave and resourceful.'

She repeated the last word silently to herself and nodded, giving a relieved little sigh.

'Just so long as he don't think I did it.'

'Didn't think you did it,' he corrected her. He put an arm around her shoulder and led her down the corridor to the cubbyhole Mrs Joe had generously given her to sleep in, as spartan a cell as Stearman had ever seen. A child's narrow bed, a battered kitchen chair and a washstand with basin and jug were all it contained. A cupboard with a single shelf held her meagre clothing and spare pair of shoes. The only items of a personal nature she had were the things Stearman had given her: a hand-mirror, hairbrush and comb, on the wall a little picture of the sea, which Lisbeth had never seen, and on the chair beside her bed, a china kitten.

He stood at the door for a minute, reassuring her that the sheriff had no interest in her.

'Things won't always be like this, Lisbeth. One day, you'll see, your whole life will change.'

'You promise?' She smiled at him, because she didn't believe a word.

'Cross my heart and hope to die,' he said. He tugged the end of her braid, then turned away to find his own bed.

Lisbeth waited till she couldn't hear his footsteps any more, then closed and locked her door and slipped into bed. She kissed the kitten goodnight and snuggled down, pressing her cold feet together for warmth.

Since the day he'd walked through the front door of Mrs Joe's rooming-house she'd taken a great shine to Mr Stearman. He was kind and generous and funny and she felt less like a friendless orphan when he was around. He was big but didn't threaten, he had a sweet smile and his eyes crinkled with a web of fine lines when he laughed. He listened to her as if she had something interesting to say even when she got her words mixed up, but most of all, she just loved the idea that he cared about her, because for sure no one else did. And it was nice of him to say that one day her life would change for the better, but it was a lie and Lisbeth knew it. She didn't mind all that much because she had never known anything else but hard knocks, hard work and poverty. Just so long as Mr Stearman stayed around a little bit longer.

CHAPTER 10

There was enough money in Randall Anderson's bundle to bury both him and what was left of Luther Rawl. After a brief, sparsely attended inquest, with a verdict of unlawful killing by person or persons unknown, they were lowered into the same grave in separate coffins.

The funeral party was a small one. Parson Finch, Sheriff Moss, Stearman, Lisbeth, Jumper the gravedigger, and Harry Barclay. Barclay was the owner of the town's only funeral business, left him by a distant relative, who'd had the foresight to buy the land that the cemetery came to be built on. Nobody got buried in Randolph without the services of Harry Barclay, be it the purchase of a coffin, which Stearman made and he sold, or a plot in the cemetery. Barclay was a tall, well-set-up man approaching fifty, dressed perpetually in sober black coats and cravats. He had a long, sad-looking face that sat well with his chosen profession and thick, well-cut white hair with a centre parting. He ran his business efficiently, treated all who came through the doors of his funeral parlour with grave respect, and considered himself fortunate to have acquired the skills of John Stearman after losing Gunter.

On that chill autumn morning the parson read the burial

service in a strong, clear voice while Lisbeth shivered in a thin shawl and cried for the stranger who had held her hand as he died. Stearman, watching her, decided to spend what was left of Anderson's money on something warm for her to wear.

After everyone had thrown a little soil down into the grave, the party split up, leaving Jumper to begin his work. Doc Moss and Parson Finch strolled away together and Stearman walked Lisbeth to the cemetery gates, but after watching her hurry back to the rooming-house, he returned to where Jumper was taking a fortifying swig from the bottle he always kept by him.

'Better not let Harry Barclay catch you,' he warned mildly. Jumper hunched his thin shoulders as the liquor scalded his alcohol-ravaged throat and burned its way down into his empty stomach. He was a man nearer fifty than forty, with sparse dark hair. He was thin, his body wasted by years of heavy drinking and little food. Some tragedy long past had caused his ruin, but Jumper had drowned his sorrows so many times that he was no longer sure of the exact details. A Southerner who'd fought for the Union, he walked with a limp that he didn't care to explain. He wore a black frock-coat and tie when the burial services were conducted, standing back a little, head respectfully bowed, and he always had a quiet, kindly word for the mourners, which, spoken in his soft Carolina drawl, served to soften them up for big a fat tip. 'That ol' tidewater charm, John. Works every time,' he'd told Stearman once.

'Nobody cares if the gravedigger's drunk,' Jumper now observed amiably. 'It's not as if I'm likely to kill anybody.'

'That's for sure.' Stearman smiled. He liked Jumper. He had no aim in life other than to stay mildly inebriated all day long. He was cheerful and contented with his lot. 'How's the arm?' he asked.

Jumper had taken a pretty bad fall about a week ago and wrenched his shoulder, had been unable to work and had been worried Harry Barclay might replace him. But for all his slightness of build and fondness for the bottle, Jumper could do the work of three other men and Barclay knew it.

'All but mended.' Jumper shrugged.

'I just came back to ask about putting up a stone on the grave.'

'I could take care of that for you, John. Know the stone-mason. Might cost a little bit, though, if you want some words on it.'

Stearman held out a slip of paper on which were written two men's names and the dates they died.

'Ask how much. One of the men left a little money to pay for it.'

He didn't want to go through Barclay for a stone. Even though he worked for him, he would charge over the odds. A chill gust of wind ruffled the sparse hair on Jumper's bare head and he grimaced up at the grey sky.

'Winter comin'. Mr Barclay will need to hire another man to help me cut the graves soon, when the ground gets too hard.'

'Rather you than me,' Stearman admitted as he hunched up his shoulders and headed back to the workshop behind the funeral parlour. He heated coffee on his little stove in the corner and drank a mugful before getting down to work with the familiar tools of his adopted trade, hammer, saw, nails and plane, shaping the cheap wood Barclay used for most of his customers with a skill that made the finished product look finer than it was.

He had been working for about an hour when he stopped to clear his floor space, reaching for the broom to sweep up the curls of wood shavings and sawdust. He liked to keep his workplace tidy.

'I'm looking for the coffin man,' a voice said from the doorway. Stearman turned to look at the woman standing there.

'You've found him,' he said. The woman took another cautious step into the room, looking with interest at the stacked wood and trestle tables bearing finished and half-finished caskets.

'Can I speak to you for a minute, sir? It's Mr Stearman, isn't it?' she asked. She was a tall girl, wearing a dark-blue dress and jacket in a cheap but serviceable material, with a white blouse underneath, a small hat of dark-blue felt and feathers, and practical half-boots, and she carried a large embroidered bag.

He indicated the corner of the workshop that he laughingly called his office: two chairs and a cheap desk, a shelf with one or two ledgers and the squat little stove on which he brewed coffee. She sat on one of the chairs, declined a cup of coffee and took a deep breath before telling him why she had come.

'I'm sorry to take you away from your work,' she said, but he inclined his head as if to say it was no matter. She had been wrong-footed by finding a younger man than she had supposed him to be and good-looking too, with a quiet, attentive manner and dark, deep-blue eyes.

'It's just that I was told that you spoke to my cousin Betsy about a week ago and I wondered if she might have mentioned to you where she was going.'

Stearman tried to remember the name, which was certainly familiar. A week ago he had been on his way back from his buying trip.

'Was she a blonde girl, blue eyes, very pretty?'

'Yes, sir, that exactly describes her. You remember speaking to her then?' the woman asked eagerly.

'I met her on the train. There was a little unpleasantness and I helped her with it, then I walked her to a hotel on Beacon Street. She said she was going to stay with her cousin.'

'Yes, that was me. I work at Ludlow's. My name is Grace Milton. She didn't say anything else, maybe, that she had some other errand to attend to first?'

'What's happened, ma'am? She didn't go into the hotel, I take it?'

'No sir, nor did she go anywhere else. She's just disappeared, like she never existed.'

For no good reason, Stearman suddenly thought of the bag belonging to the man on the train. He had kicked it under the bed the night Randall Anderson turned up and had forgotten all about it. But the girl's tormentor could not have made it into town in time to harm her that night, could he?

'You said there was some unpleasantness on the train, sir?' she asked and he re-focused on her.

She looked older than her cousin; he gauged her to be in her mid-twenties. She had washed-out, slightly careworn prettiness: bright, warm blue eyes, high cheekbones, a sweet, full lower lip and a little cleft in her chin. She looked like a girl used to hard work and plenty of it, and a life with few pleasures.

'There was a man on the train, wanted to sit with her, but started to get a little too friendly, so I persuaded him to leave her alone.'

'Persuaded him?'

'I suggested he get off the train when we stopped to take on water,' said Stearman with a rueful smile. 'We were about eight, maybe ten miles out, so I don't think he would have been a danger to her, even if he managed to get a ride into town.'

'I went to see a friend of hers, from when she used to work here in town, but she hadn't seen her. Then I sent a wire to the family she works for in Lydia, but they sent back word that she hadn't gone home. Then I went to see Doc Moss.'

'What did he say?'

'He asked a lot of questions and said that he'd try to find out what happened, but I could tell he just thought she had gone off with some young man. But Betsy wasn't like that. She was a steady girl, not at all flighty.'

'You must be worried sick,' he observed softly, and her eyes suddenly filled with tears, throwing Stearman into complete confusion. She fumbled in her bag for a handkerchief and quickly blotted the tears away, then gave him a watery smile.

'I'm so sorry, but you were my last hope. Someone from the hotel told me they saw you speaking to her that night and I just thought. . . .'

'She only said she was going into the hotel, nothing else. I wish I could tell you more. You said she used to work here in Randolph? Who did she work for?'

'It was in the house of Councilman Parry and his wife. She was a housemaid there. And she was quite friendly with their cook, Mrs Cobb.'

She noticed the look on Stearman's face at the mention of Parry's name, but didn't know what it meant. 'She worked there for about a year, then one day she came and told me she'd had a better offer from a family in Lydia. Said she didn't get on with Mrs Parry, so she wanted a change. I was sorry to see her go. She's just about the only kin I have left in this part of the world.'

'You're not local to Randolph?' he asked.

'No, sir. My family come from Pennsylvania. I came here with my father when I was twelve or so. He worked on the railroad. When this section was finished, we settled here. But he died about five years ago. Betsy's parents came out a little later than us, but they died same time as my father. It was a bad 'flu that year, killed a lot of people.'

Suddenly aware that she had been running on, giving him her life story when he was probably not at all interested, she blushed and shook her head. 'Well anyway, I'm obliged to you for taking care of her on the train. That was good of you.'

He shook his head. He had been glad to help, would do it again; if only he had waited till the girl had gone inside. But where in the world had she gone? Miss Milton stood up, gathering her bag, composing herself. She wanted to stay and talk some more but she had slipped out of the hotel on her dinner-break and needed to get back. She offered her hand to him and when he took it, he found that it was icy cold.

'Thank you, Mr Stearman.'

'I'm sorry,' he said, wanting suddenly to chafe her hand with his own warm one. 'If I can think of anything else I'll let you know.'

She didn't speak again, just squeezed his work-roughened hand and turned away. Stearman followed her to the doorway and watched till she was out of sight. Then he went in search of Jumper.

The little cabin where the gravedigger kept his tools was sited up at the back of the cemetery, out of sight. Inside it contained a little pot-bellied stove; Jumper's various digging implements, none of them clean, were thrown in a jumble into a corner, the whole place smelling of damp soil, sweat and stale liquor. Jumper was slumped in a rickety, spoke-backed chair, his hands cupped around a half-empty bottle. Without waking him, Stearman lifted the bottle and looked at the label. Blackstrap. That was what had been familiar about Anderson's killer, the smell of molasses on his breath when they grappled in Anderson's room, the same drink that Jumper favoured. He returned the bottle and quietly let himself out, returning to his work.

After supper that night, he dug the bag out from under the bed, opened it and one by one removed the contents. There was about ten foot of thin-stranded rope, two butcher's boning knives, each about ten inches in length, a tightly corked bottle of clear liquid, two clean shirts and a dog-eared, much-thumbed Bible. There was a little pouch tucked in a fold of the lining, containing pictures of dance-hall girls wearing not much of anything, and two bills, one for a pair of boots costing fourteen dollars and one from a rooming-house in Lydia.

They were both made out to a man called Tipper.

CHAPTER 11

Jackson Parry owned a fine two-storey house on Brewer Street, in the prosperous north-east corner of town, where all the up-and-coming folks lived, including Harry Barclay. Stearman arrived at the front door an hour later, having changed into a clean shirt, his best boots and a good-quality single-breasted black coat that just reached his knee. He was admitted to the house by a middle-aged woman with a thin face, her hair severely restrained under a frilled cap. She had him wait in a large room, gloomy and over-furnished. The fire was unlit and was almost as chilly as his own little attic room.

Parry kept him waiting for almost twenty minutes, long enough for Stearman to give plenty of thought to how a lowly sergeant, briefly turned marauder, could afford to live in this mausoleum. When Parry finally arrived, Stearman recognized him at once from those brief minutes at the ferry. He recalled a powerfully built man, not very tall with a florid sort of handsomeness, bright blue eyes, pink cheeks and blue-black hair, worn long then.

He was heavier now, was the first thing Stearman saw, especially around the jaw and waistline. His hair was clipped short and he had grown a neat goatee beard. His clothes were expensive, his loose-sleeved linen shirt was of the best quality, a gold watch chain across his silk waistcoat. This was the self-styled Major Parry, Councilman Parry, perfectly at home in this elaborate, luxurious setting. He regarded his visitor with guarded curiosity.

'Forgive me for keeping you waiting,' he began smoothly, though he offered no explanation for the delay. 'How may I help you, Mr. . .?'

'Stearman. John Stearman.' He waited a moment to see if Parry would remember him but saw no recognition in his eyes.

'Oh yes, you work for Barclay, don't you? You're the coffin maker.'

'That's right,' Stearman replied, wondering why his occupation should cause the smirk on Parry's face. 'I'm trying to find out what happened to a young woman I met a week ago. I understand she used to work for you.'

'You're speaking of Betsy Ross, I believe,' Parry said, looking none too pleased at the mention of her name. 'We've already had her cousin here, Mr Stearman. I see no need of a further interrogation.'

Stearman did a silent summing-up of Councilman Parry then. He might walk and talk and dress like a gentleman, he might live at the smartest address in the upcoming town of Randolph, but he was still just a barrack-room bully, the kind of loud-mouthed soldier who got things done with threats and intimidation, and had only marginal control over his own temper.

'She worked for you for a year, is that correct?' Stearman asked patiently, ignoring Parry's last remark. Parry sighed and turned towards a circular table bearing a drinks decanter and glasses. He poured himself something amber-coloured.

He turned back with the drink in his hand, pointedly not offering Stearman anything.

'She worked for *my wife* for a year. I barely noticed her,' he said, adopting a wide-legged stance in front of the fireplace. 'What's your interest anyway, Stearman?'

'I spoke to her the night she disappeared and her cousin came to me to ask if she had given me any idea where she might be going.'

'And had she?' Parry asked, looking down into his glass. Stearman saw a glint of something in his eyes for a second but couldn't say for sure what it was. When Stearman didn't answer, Parry looked up at him, the beginnings of a grin on his face. 'Or did she offer to warm your bed for you and then not show up? That it, Stearman? She was well known for that, you know.'

'Is that why she left here after a year, Major?' Stearman asked, surprised by the cold fury that gripped him. 'Did she get tired of another middle-aged man breathing down her neck?'

At that moment Parry looked mad enough to kill and Stearman's undue stress on the word 'Major' was not lost on him. He put his glass down with a thump on the mantelpiece and walked to the door.

'I think you've outstayed your welcome, sir,' he said as he opened the door. Stearman didn't move for a few seconds, then strolled out of the room, his coolness causing Parry's shirt collar to tighten around his indignant neck. The door slammed behind him and, as if she had been waiting for her cue, the thin-faced maid came hurrying to let him out, looking at him wonderingly, for there weren't many who would risk rousing the major's temper.

Stearman started to walk home. Easing a finger under his necktie, working it loose, he reflected that though he had actually come up here to speak to the cook, Mrs Cobb, on the whole he felt he had learned just as much by speaking to Councilman Parry.

CHAPTER 12

Randall Anderson's killer got into the rooming-house exactly the same way as before, easing the front door open by lifting the handle, which bypassed the loose-fitting lock. Inside all was dark. Even the lamp generally left alight in the hallway was out. He climbed carefully, slowly, first floor, second floor, right turn, then the steep little stairs up to the attic rooms. Here was where he had made his mistake before, blundering into the wrong room. Still, he had taken care of the big guy, even though he seemed to have been expecting something, had been fully dressed and had a gun, which he never got a chance to use. He wouldn't get it wrong tonight.

Stearman had gone out earlier and the intruder knew he didn't have much time to do what he had to do before he returned. The man who followed him and watched him through the window had been told he often worked late. Smallpox in Canvas Town, influenza in the west end of town, it all meant extra work for Stearman.

The lock on the door at the top of the house opened easily, one twist of the picklock and he was in. He closed the door quietly behind him. The room was much darker than the other room had been and after a time he realized why.

76

There was a heavy curtain over the window, blocking out every bit of light and rendering the room pitch black. He moved cautiously across the floor and reached up to draw the covering aside, but found that it was only resting on the curtain rail, not attached to it. He puzzled over that for a fatal five seconds before pulling the curtain down, letting in enough light to let him search. He turned round and standing behind the door, with a Colt revolver in his hand, was John Stearman. Doc Moss was sitting in a chair in the corner, holding the bag the intruder had come to find. He had walked into a very neat little trap.

'Where's the knife?' Stearman asked him.

'I don't know—'

'The knife you used to kill Randall Anderson when you went into the wrong room last week.' Stearman cut off his protest. A flare of light distracted the intruder. Doc Moss had lit the lamp on the bedside table and Stearman saw what he already knew, that the intruder was the man he had put off the train.

'I just wanted my bag back. You said you'd leave it at the ticket office.'

'I forgot,' Stearman said, deadpan. 'Now give me that knife you've got in your boot and sit down.'

The intruder was about to pull an innocent 'What knife?' but thought better of it and bent to pull the blade out, slowly, watchful of Stearman, who looked as if he would like nothing better than to pull the trigger. He tossed it on to the bed where Stearman indicated and then sat down on the chair by the table, exactly where Randall Anderson had sat last week. He put his hands on the table without needing to be told, though he wanted to wipe the sweat from his face. The room was cold but he could feel the heat of his own fear on his skin.

'Is your name Tipper?' Doc Moss asked. Again the man hesitated, gauging how far a lie would get him and deciding not far enough.

'Yeah,' he mumbled, realizing they had found the bill for the rooming-house.

'Now, son, me and Mr Stearman here would like to know what purpose you would have for a bag like this.'

'It's just my work bag,' he answered with a shrug.

'What kind of work?' Doc asked without any inflection or rancour, just three men having a little conversation. 'I mean to say, what kind of work involves boning knives, ropes and chloroform?'

'Don't bother trying to think up some feeble answer. We all know what the bag is for. Now tell us what you did with that little girl before I toss your worthless hide out of that window,' Stearman warned him, stepping forward so that he blocked Doc Moss's view.

'John,' the sheriff said softly, Stearman sighed and moved to one side, sitting down on the foot of the bed so that he faced Tipper across the little table.

'Mr Stearman tells me you made a pest of yourself with a young woman on the train a week ago.'

'I was just having a little fun with her. Didn't mean her no harm,' Tipper whined, trying to look innocent, but all he achieved was an ugly squinting leer on his long face.

'The young woman has gone missing,' Doc told him and Tipper's brain laboriously made the connection.

'Well, it weren't me. I never seen her after he put me off the train. How could I? He left me in the middle of nowhere. I had to wait till morning in that ol' shed till the first train came in the morning and it was going in the other direction. Train took me back to where I started. I just got back here two days ago.'

'And that's when you came looking for your bag?' Moss asked him.

'I didn't mean to hurt him.'

'You hurt him all right. He's dead and buried,' Stearman observed harshly.

'I just wanted what was mine but he came at me like a crazy madman. I was just defending myself.'

Stearman and Moss looked at one another. It would be easy enough to prove that he had been on that morning train, which would pretty much clear him of having anything to do with whatever had happened to Betsy that night. But he had well and truly incriminated himself with regard to Randall Anderson.

'A jury might well well agree with you, Mr Tipper. I'm not sure I do,' Doc Moss said. 'In any event, you're under arrest for the murder of Randall Anderson and I'd like you to come along with me now.'

He came quietly enough, and after they had locked him up for the night in the cells, Doc Moss settled into his office chair, a very old swivel with a red leather seat, the arms rubbed smooth with age. It creaked like an old friend when he turned to where Stearman was sitting, on the hard wooden bench kept against the wall. It was almost midnight and the street beyond the half-painted windows was quiet. In the sheriff's office, the wall clock ticked and a pan of water on the stove in the corner came to the boil.

Stearman didn't like being awake at this hour. His mind started to worry on things, fretting at the past like it was an old wound that ached in the rain. He found himself going back to places and people he never thought about in the busy daylight hours.

'I'm sorry I never came to you that night, when I got off the train,' he said. 'I intended to, first thing in the morning, but when I got back to my room, Randall Anderson was waiting for me and I've been chasing his ghosts ever since. I even forgot the bag until tonight.'

'Well, we got him for killing your friend, anyway.'

'But we still don't know what happened to the girl.'

'In the last two years five other girls have gone missing, did you know that?'

Stearman shook his head.

'Well, you wouldn't because they all came from Canvas Town, all poor, unconnected, faceless girls, all aged from about twelve to twenty. Three of them weren't missed for nigh on to a month.'

'You think Betsy Ross is one of these missing girls?'

'I think she might be. I think we'll have to get our Mr Tipper to start talking, tell us who his accomplice is.'

Stearman had been thinking along the same lines.

'I tried to find the conductor when the train pulled into the station, but there was no sign of him.'

'I already made one or two enquiries on that. Seems the guard felt poorly, left the train at Lydia. The last train of the day doesn't go any further than Randolph, just pulls into a siding a little ways west of town and lays up for the night, so he didn't feel too bad leaving because the train only had one more stop. Whether he was genuinely ill or not, I don't know.'

'Tipper said he'd paid the guard to stay away. Betsy's cousin came by the workshop to see me, asked if I had any idea what happened to the girl.'

'Grace Milton? She the girl works at Ludlow's? Well, don't tell her any of this yet, John. Let's pray for a miracle. Let's pray Betsy's still alive. There'll be plenty of time to give her the bad news when we know what it is.'

Stearman nodded agreement, then gave a huge yawn that

quickly affected the sheriff.

'Damn it, John, don't start that,' Doc said, giving his head a shake. He got up to brew the coffee and brought Stearman a mug of it, thick and tarry and aromatic. They drank and talked a little more, then Stearman got up to go, stretching his big frame tiredly. He said 'Goodnight' as he headed for the door.

'You'll let me know, if he says anything?' he asked at the door, nodding towards the back of the room, beyond which the cells were situated.

'Count on it,' Doc Moss assured him.

CHAPTER 13

Stearman was up and ready to leave early in the morning without waiting for breakfast when Mrs Joe stopped him at the foot of the stairs and begged a few minutes of his time in her private apartments. He followed her into the back room, which was a small space, her sitting room and office in one, the big roll-top desk jostling for space with a button-back sofa in red plush and two upholstered, overstuffed chairs. A hand-tinted likeness of her late husband hung above the desk, gloomily overseeing her accounts and correspondence. She sat down with a creak of corsets, arranging herself regally, her hands clasped on her lap.

She did not invite Stearman to sit. She began by asking him if he would be so good as to vacate his room as soon as possible as he was no longer suitable as a tenant. She was very sorry to give him such short notice but she had her other boarders to think of.

Taken by surprise at first, Stearman quickly recovered and listened to her in silence until she had exhausted all her excuses. He had brought disrepute to her respectable establishment with his sordid behaviour, brawling in the corridors at night, dragging Lisbeth into it so that the child was scared half to death, and then what next but the sheriff is on her

82

premises in the middle of the night to arrest another of his unsavoury friends. It wasn't to be tolerated. All her friends said that she was too soft on her tenants, that she let them get away with murder, and she could not stand by and let Stearman drag her late husband's good name in the dirt.

She had worked herself into a nicely gauged lather when Stearman took a step towards her and suddenly gripped her by the arm, just above the elbow. He yanked her, good and hard, out of her chair. He heard her teeth rattle with the force of it. Her eyes bulged and her mouth opened but no sound came out.

'I never knew anyone who liked the sound of their own voice as much as you do,' he said in a soft, menacing tone, his lips close to her ear. 'You've had a visit from somebody about me, haven't you?'

She turned a headshake of denial into a nod when she saw the look on his face.

'Was it Councilman Parry? What did he say?'

'He said my licence to run this house was about up for renewal and if I wanted to keep the place running I'd better do like he said.'

'Get rid of me?'

'I'm not stupid enough to cross him.'

'Well, I certainly wouldn't want to get you into any trouble,' he said drily, still keeping an iron grip on her arm. Up close she didn't smell so clean. 'Listen to me very carefully. When I walk out of that door you don't take it out on Lisbeth and if I see that girl with another bruise or burn, I'll come after you, and ma'am, I don't like to be crossed either. As of today, you start to pay her for her week's work, and you hire some more help. She's overworked and stretched to the limit, while you sit in here drinking gin all day.'

He released her arm and she stumbled away from him,

dropping back down on to her chair with hatred burning in her eyes.

'How dare you,' she hissed, floundering like most bullies when their bluff is called. Her attempt at fierce outrage produced no more than a puff of hot air.

'It's just a question of who you fear most, Parry or me.'

It took him less than ten minutes to pack his gear and leave the attic room forever. He decided he wouldn't quibble over the few days remaining on the rent he had paid. Let her have it. He did want a word with Lisbeth before leaving, though, but she wasn't to be found by the time he walked out of the rooming-house, his bag over his shoulder. He was about to cross the street when he heard his name called. He turned to see Lisbeth standing in the lane that ran along the side of the rooming-house. He could tell by the look on her face that she knew what had happened. She twisted her red, work-roughened hands together and stared at him like a puppy headed for the pound. With a hand on her shoulder he turned her slightly, shielding her from the cutting October wind with his body.

'I'm so sorry, Mr Stearman.'

'It's all right, Lisbeth. I'll find another place.'

'Why did she want you to go? You're the only one ever pays the rent on time. Was it something to do with that poor man that died?' she asked.

'Something like that. But I made a deal with her and from now on she's going to pay you a fair wage for all the work you do. How does that sound?'

Lisbeth's eyes widened, but not with pleasure or gratitude.

'You shouldn't have done that, Mr Stearman,' she said anxiously, shaking her head. 'She never lets anybody get the better of her. She'll find a way to get back at me.'

How many times, Stearman wondered, had something hard and heavy come down on this girl's head, killing all her hopes and aspirations, till she had now reached the point where a piece of good news was instantly turned into bad. He couldn't begin to know what her life had been before he knew her, but it must have been pretty bad if she thought living as an unpaid drudge with Mrs Joe was her best option.

'Lisbeth, if she does anything bad to you I want you to go to somebody I know. Her name is Miss Milton and she works at the Ludlow Hotel on Beacon Street. She'll look out for you. Will you do that for me?'

Stearman didn't know where he pulled that name from but somehow it felt right.

'But who'll look after you now? Who'll take care of your laundry and sew on your buttons and make sure you eat breakfast? And you know, when you go to Wheatley's for whiskey sometimes and lock your door for two days, who's gonna make sure you eat something? That was my job,' Lisbeth gently reminded him.

Stearman looked momentarily stricken. All this time, while he thought he had been Lisbeth's protector, it had been the other way round. This slight young girl, with no family and no home and little future, had watched over and cared for him as if he was her responsibility and he hadn't even noticed. She had taken the wind right out of his sails. He let her go and then pulled her gently towards him to give her a hug.

'Remember what I said the other night, that one of these days things would get better?' He felt her nod though she didn't speak. 'I meant what I said. I'm going to find a place for you, a better place than this. I have some things to do right now, but I'll get it all sorted out.' He let her go and bent down to lift the bag he had rested at his feet. He reached inside and withdrew a small parcel wrapped in brown paper. 'I forgot to give you this when I got back from my trip the other day.'

She opened it up and saw inside a bunch of pretty hair-ribbons, a dozen or more, folded inside the paper. Her face lit up with pleasure as she examined the pink and lavender and scarlet but when she looked up to thank him, Stearman was gone, walking purposefully down the street towards the workshop. She waved as he turned the corner but he didn't see her.

CHAPTER 14

He went straight to the workshop, deciding to leave finding a place to stay till later in the day. He tossed his bag into a corner, put on his work apron and set to, taking out all his frustration on several blameless pieces of pinewood, sawing and hammering and planing them into shape with fierce concentration. He was thinking about how best to deal with Councilman Parry when he had a visitor.

Harry Barclay strolled into the workshop, his fists in his pockets, looking even more doleful than usual, gazing around with an abstracted air.

'It always surprises me how tidy you keep things,' he commented. 'The place was always hip deep in sawdust and shavings when Gunter worked here.'

Stearman put down the chisel he had been using and straightened up, wondering what had brought his employer here this morning. He could count on one hand the number of times he had visited the workshop in two years.

'Something I can help you with, Harry?'

Barclay rested his hip on the corner of a trestle and folded his arms, cleared his throat and refused to meet Stearman's eye. Suddenly Stearman knew why he had come.

'Let me guess, you've had a visit from Councilman Parry.'

Barclay looked at him then, and Stearman saw that he was steeling himself to speak about something unpleasant.

'That jumped-up little toe-rag! He's no more a major than Jumper. Coming here, telling me how to run my business.'

'What did he threaten you with?'

'Everything he could think of, John, what the hell did you do to get him so fired up?'

'Asked him a couple of questions about a girl who's gone missing. She used to work for him.'

Barclay knew Parry. He had a dangerous temper and a long memory and no one crossed him who wanted to prosper in this town.

'I'm sorry, John. He's got some pretty powerful friends. For the time being at least I have to let you go, though the good Lord knows how I'll replace you.'

Stearman couldn't believe what he was hearing. He stared at Barclay as if staring could help him grow a backbone, then he gave his characteristic little shrug, the merest lift of one shoulder, and smoothed his hand along the edge of the last coffin he would ever make.

'I'll need half an hour to square away and pack my gear,' he said tonelessly, removing his leather work-apron.

'Take as long as you need, John. And if there's anything I can do to help, you let me know,' Barclay said, without a hint of irony. 'Come round to the office. I'll have your wages made up.' He turned away with his head bowed and his hands shoved deep in his pockets, looking less like a man who has undertaken a difficult and painful task than a man who has unloaded himself of a troublesome burden. In the yard he stopped to call to Jumper to come see him in the front office when he was finished what he was doing. Stearman gathered up his tools and put them away in the toolbox Gunter had left him. He had just pulled on his coat when Jumper appeared in the doorway.

'Finishing up for the day, John?' he asked.

'Finished up for good.'

'How come? What do you mean?'

'Seems Mr Barclay no longer requires my services.'

Jumper stared at him as if he had been given the most complex problem in the universe to solve. Stearman was the best carpenter they'd ever had, he was cheap and hardworking and he didn't even seem to drink much. Yet Harry Barclay was firing him.

'I don't get it,' he said. 'Is Mr Barclay selling up or something?'

'Jumper, what do you know about Councilman Parry?' Stearman asked. Jumper squeezed his lower lip and stared down at the floor, frowning.

'What I hear is he knows where all the bodies are buried. He's got the dirt on just about everybody in this town and he knows how to use it. He wants a saloon on every corner and wants to do away with the sheriff's 'no gun' rule. Says it's bad for business. You crossed his path, John?'

'We had a few words. But he might find he's not the only one who knows where the bodies are buried.'

'You steer clear of him. He's bad news, and he doesn't always pay others to take care of his dirty work. Likes to get his hands in it himself sometimes, so I'm told.'

'Thanks for the advice,' Stearman said without rancour. He dug his bag out of the corner where he had thrown it this morning and turned to find Jumper pulling stuff out of pockets, bits of paper, coins, string, and at least three keys. He returned most of the items to his pockets, but held out one of the crumpled scraps of paper.

'What's this?' Stearman took it and smoothed it out. It

89

had a jumble of numbers written on it.

'That's a quote from the stonemason, for putting the names on that headstone, like you asked me.'

'I forgot. I'll go see him. Thanks, Jumper.'

Jumper ducked his head like an old turtle, in a way that had become familiar to Stearman and with a little nod turned to walk away. Then paused at the door.

'I'm sorry you're leaving, John. Maybe I could put in a word for you with Harry,' he offered.

Stearman smiled but shook his head. Jumper walked on. Stearman looked down at the piece of paper in his hand. Something had happened in the last ten minutes that was important, relevant somehow. He reviewed what Barclay and Jumper had said and done, but couldn't put a finger on it. Not then, anyway.

CHAPTER 15

Doc Moss, taking a leisurely turn around the town, spotted a familiar figure, walking towards him, loaded down with bag and toolbox.

'That's a lazy man's load you've got there, John. Not thinking about leaving town, I hope? You promised me your finest pine box as I recall. What's going on?'

He watched as Stearman lowered the bag and box and eased his back with both hands.

'Well, I lost my job and my room at Mrs Joe's, so I thought I'd head on over to your office to see if you wanted to arrest me. Put the finishing touch to my day.'

Doc Moss was for once lost for words. He favoured Stearman with an unblinking stare, patted various pockets and, for added measure, scratched his jaw.

'Not many men in town got that much clout. Would we be speaking of a certain councilman?'

'He seems to have taken exception to my questions the other night about Betsy Ross.'

'Well, let's get you organized. We're blocking traffic here.'

The sheriff stooped to pick up Stearman's bag, leaving him to carry his workbox. With a tilt of his head, he motioned for him to follow. He led the way to his house, which stood right at the west end of town, a narrow, two-storey building, set a little back from the road. He had lived here since his marriage to his wife, Mary, who had been dead these last five years. The house was neat and old-fashioned in the best possible way, simply but comfortably furnished and as clean as might be.

'It's too big for me now all the boys are grown, but I guess it'll see me out,' he said as Stearman looked about appreciatively. 'You can have any room but mine. I sleep at the front. Stow your gear and come down. I'll fix the coffee.'

He walked off to the kitchen before Stearman could thank him, so he lifted his bag and climbed the stairs. One small bedroom looked over a long, narrow, well-tended garden area at the back, with a big tree close to the house that cast dappled shadow on the bedroom wall. It had a big bed, not like the jail-cell cot at Dora Forbes's place, and white-painted drawers and washstand. There was a comfortable chair in the corner beside a fireplace, which his other room had also lacked.

He left his bag and met up with Doc Moss in the kitchen, where coffee was brewing. The sheriff brought the pot from the range to the table and poured it, good, hot and strong, into his wife's second-best china and offered sugar and milk and a plate of sour-cream biscuits.

Stearman sat down at the table and they ate and drank in silence for a time while the clock on the kitchen wall ticked chestily and outside one of Doc's neighbours chopped kindling with a rhythmic thunk-thunk.

'I'd like nothing better than to throw Councilman Parry's sorry hide in my jail,' Doc began, but Stearman shook his head.

'I don't want you to go near him. Let him think he's won.

I'll deal with Sergeant Parry when the time is right.'

'By deal with him you mean what, exactly?'

'I'll let you know when I've worked out the finer details. But if I allow a little barrack-room bully like Jack Parry to reorder my life, then I'm not the man my father raised.'

'You've got him worried about something, that's for sure.'

'And I intend to find out what.'

'You know, Mr Lincoln once said: "Nearly all men can stand adversity but if you want to test a man's character give him power." Councilman Parry's been given a little power and I think we can see what his character is.'

'Personally I wouldn't put him in charge of feeding the hogs.'

'As an officer of the law I feel it my bounden duty to warn you not to interfere in my business,' Doc said in his most serious tone. 'But as I'm overworked and underpaid I'll take all the help I can get.'

Doc poured more coffee and leaned back in his chair, his eyes touching on the much-loved things of his wife's. In this kitchen he had stolen kisses, squeezed an ample hip, watched her frown in concentration when she fried his bacon. He'd felt the sting of her dishrag when he teased her and enjoyed her laughter when he amused her. He'd eaten her meat loaf and pot roast and the smell of cinnamon still brought her wondrously to life for him. He'd dried her tears and listened to her concerns, just as she had lovingly listened to his, and he had wanted to spend all eternity with her. This room, more than any other in the house, had been hers and this was where he felt closest to her.

As to why he had brought John Stearman back here? Doc pressed a thumb to his neat moustache and looked at his new house guest, who was making inroads on the biscuits his housekeeper Mrs Terrell had baked for him. He liked

Stearman with an unreserved liking that surprised him. He was a man carrying a big burden, so heavy it dragged on every muscle in his body, bowed his shoulders, left him without room or energy for anything else, and Doc wanted him to just let it go, whatever it was from his past or the war, whatever, put it down and leave it behind him.

'I'm sorry all this has happened to you, John.'

'I feel like somebody's roped me to the back of an express train. Turned my life inside out, that's for sure.'

'I have a notion it's not the life you thought you'd be living,' Doc surmised shrewdly. Stearman took a while to answer, lost in thought, turning over a few memories before he sighed, drained his coffee cup and held it out for a refill.

'Nobody lives the life they thought they would, Doc.'

'I guess that's true, son.'

'Listen, thanks for the room. I'll try not to get in your hair for too long.'

'Stay as long as you want. House is so damn quiet sometimes, I'll be glad of a little company. With all my boys gone and now my Mary, too, it gets a little quiet around here,'

'How many boys?' Stearman asked.

'Three, two married, living back East. My eldest stayed in the army at the end of the war. He's out West somewhere, Arizona last time he wrote. He's the one his mother always worried about. And the one I miss the most. Shouldn't be that way, I know. Man shouldn't have favourites amongst his sons, but Jay was mine. I hope he'll come back someday.'

The sheriff had surprised himself, talking like this about his family to someone he didn't know that well, but as he glanced up at Stearman, at the interested, thoughtful look on his face, he knew it was because he reminded him of his eldest boy. Like Jay he was fathoms deep, quiet, capable. He was the man you wanted at your side when trouble showed up.

'And this way I can keep an eye on you,' he said, surprising Stearman.

'I won't go up against Parry without letting you know first,' Stearman said, drawing entirely the wrong conclusion from Doc's words. 'Though I might not need the room for a day or two. Now that I'm a man of leisure I'm going to take time to try to find Hobie. I owe him that much for what he did for me. Maybe Luther's and Randall's deaths had nothing to do with the ferry and maybe they did, but I'd like to give him a little warning just in case.'

'Maybe there's something you could do for me at the same time,' the sheriff suggested tentatively. 'Maybe you could go to Lydia and have a word with the family Betsy Ross worked for. The husband came here and asked around but maybe his wife or other family members know something that could help.'

'Can't hurt. Be glad to.'

'I'll stand any expense you might run to. Got a little fund for that kind of thing. And I can spare one of the deputies if you want? Mel or Frank'd be happy to go.'

'No, sir, thank you anyway. Think I might get along better on my own.' Stearman stood to go. 'I need to do one more thing before I leave, though.'

At Ludlow's Hotel he asked for Miss Milton, received a frown of disapproval from the starchy desk clerk and stood stolidly by the counter when told to take a seat while the clerk enquired. Miss Milton came a few minutes later, her face warm from the work she had been undertaking, drying her hands on her apron, and looking worried and hopeful all at once.

Stearman removed his hat when he saw her, noticing that her hair was a dark auburn and, though tied neatly back and pinned to the back of her head, was inclined to curl. As she drew close to him, he could smell lye soap and guessed she had been working in the laundry room.

'Have you got some news for me?' she asked a bit breathlessly. Stearman shook his head and smiled an apology.

'I'm sorry, ma'am, no news yet.' She sighed and indicated two chairs behind the door where they could sit for a moment to talk. The desk clerk cleared his throat and glanced at the clock over his shoulder, but she ignored him and sat down with her body turned slightly towards Stearman, so that the clerk was blocked from view.

He took off his hat, ran his fingers through his hair and leaned back in the chair, crossing one leg over the other. The girl thought he was graceful, for a big man, and his hair reminded her of bracken, with its thick twists of brown and gold. Her heart was beating a little faster because he was sitting so close.

'What can I do for you, Mr Stearman?' she asked him. He turned to look at her and just kept on looking till she felt her colour rising. She found herself suppressing an urge to laugh with pleasure.

'I have to go away for a few days and I wondered if I might beg a favour.'

'Go on and ask.' She smiled.

'There's a young girl who works for Dora Forbes. I used to board there and I've always kept a bit of an eye on her. Her name is Lisbeth. I told her that if anything should happen while I'm away, she should come to you.'

'You mean the little lame girl? Yes, I know her. We meet sometimes in Wheatley's store. What kind of thing do you think might happen?'

'Mrs Joe has a mean streak a yard wide. I would just like to know that Lisbeth has a friend other than me.'

'I would try to get her a place with me but it probably isn't much better here,' Miss Milton said, looking at the clerk, and at the lobby with its tired air of shabby respectability.

'At least they pay you,' Stearman pointed out, and the girl's eyes widened in surprise.

'She doesn't get paid? How can Mrs Joe get away with that? Why, it's all but slavery.'

Stearman shrugged and gave her another of those long, slow looks that made her feel as if she was being slowly scorched. He looked at her hair and eyes and her throat, which was damp with cooling perspiration, and then back to her eyes. She raised a hand to the neck of her dress, where the top button was undone, flustered by his interest.

'Tell Lisbeth she can come to me any time, if she needs to,' she said. He nodded to himself and stood up to go, looking down at her for a moment, tapping his hat against his thigh.

'Already did,' he said. Her mouth opened on a half-hearted protest, but then he smiled at her and she forgave him his presumption. His words were not spoken in arrogance but in a simple belief that she was a good person and that she would help Lisbeth if she could.

CHAPTER 16

He had come to look for Hobie but Hobie wasn't to be found. After a two-hour train ride to the town of Dansing and a quick bite to eat in a clean little luncheon room on the main street, Stearman had quartered the town, asking everybody he could think of where he could find the boy. He did find out that Hobie had lived with his grandfather and aunt on a smallholding three miles up the turnpike till about six months ago, but that his folks had died of the diphtheria. There were several versions of this: that only the grandfather had died, or both relations or, in at least one telling, that Hobie had died too. This version involved a long and rambling tale of how the town had been quarantined when the diphtheria broke out, with armed guards on the main roads and trains not allowed to stop, but the disease had died out and hadn't been near as bad as in the epidemic of '53.

Stearman had patiently allowed the story to run its course, thanked the man who told him, but was really no further on with his search. Later he found out that Hobie had sold the farm and moved into town, but where he lived or what he did to earn his living was shrouded in mystery. Stearman had started to think that no one wanted to tell him about Hobie.

His last port of call before catching the train back to Randolph was the sheriff's office. Sheriff Grover was a redhead, with a crop of freckles and a smile that didn't reach his pale, watchful eyes. But he welcomed Stearman with a handshake and invited him to sit in the visitor's chair in front of his desk.

'You're looking for a friend, you say?' he asked.

'His name is Walter Hobart, though I believe everybody calls him Hobie. I promised a friend I'd look him up if I was in the area.'

'I know the family. The two older relatives died some months past. We had an outbreak of diphtheria here, real bad time for us. But I don't know where Hobie is right now. He got a job with the grain merchant for a while, but I think he moved on.'

Stearman scratched his cheek and wondered why the hell everybody was lying to him.

'Too bad. He did me a good turn right at the end of the war and I never got the chance to thank him.'

The sheriff tapped a pencil on the desk surface and gave Stearman a long, intense look.

'Sounds like Hobie all right. He's pretty well thought of around here.'

'Well, thank you for your time, Sheriff. Seems like I've reached a dead end.'

The sheriff stood up to walk Stearman to the door, looking quietly pleased with himself. He opened the door and wished him a pleasant trip back to wherever he had come from.

As the door closed behind him, Stearman shook his head and put a hand up to squeeze the back of his neck in frustration. He was missing something here. He turned on his heel to look back into Grover's office, and saw the sheriff putting some papers into a cabinet in a corner. Then something caught his eye, on the wall to his right. There was a noticeboard with information pinned to it, about church socials, lost dogs, items for sale, rooms to let and suchlike. But right in the middle, there was a notice he read with particular interest. Stearman glanced at Grover, still poking things into the cabinet, and then neatly removed the handbill and stowed it in his coat pocket.

It was time to go home. As he turned towards the railroad station he came to the conclusion that if nobody in this entire town knew where Hobie was then probably the man who had killed the Rawl brothers and possibly Phil Hunter didn't know where he was either.

He pulled his collar up and held it shut with one hand as he walked back to the station, his other hand deep in the pocket of his coat. He stepped off one boardwalk and crossed the street to another and turned the last corner, with the buildings of the station in sight. Then the attack came.

Two men came out of the alley just ahead of him and another two came up behind. He felt the jab of the gun barrel in his back, then he was manhandled back into the alley and was marched its length to a lane behind the buildings, where a horse and wagon stood waiting.

It all happened in seconds. Stearman had been wrong-footed by the speed of it, as neat an ambush as he had ever seen. The four men were muffled to the eyes, with hats jammed low and collars turned up. There were three big men, as tall and well-built as Stearman, and one smaller man who wanted to talk but was ordered to shut up more than once by his friends. At the wagon they bound Stearman, wrists and ankles, and a coarse scarf was wound tight around his face, covering eyes, nose and mouth. He was tossed into the back of the cart and covered with a horse blanket. After a low-whispered dialogue conversation between themselves, three of the men climbed in around him and the fourth sat up on the driver's seat.

The rig moved off with a jerk. Stearman struggled to breathe through the gag and tried to shift one of his arms, which was trapped underneath him and hurting. His movements annoyed the others and one of them kicked him just above the knee, warning him in a disguised growl to 'be still'.

As they jounced along Stearman, hot and sweating and uncomfortable under the blanket, had time to wonder where this was leading. He was encouraged by the fact that they were covered up and had tried to disguise their voices. That meant he might live. He felt sure in his mind that Jack Parry had organized this. Who else could it be? Nobody would suspect the major to have had any part in it, not this far from Randolph. If he did live, Stearman vowed, there would be a reckoning between him and the phoney major.

They rattled along for what might have been half an hour or longer, the road initially fairly smooth then becoming increasingly ridged and rutted and pot-holed. Stearman tossed back and forth on the wagon bed, his head twice cracking hard against the sideboard. It was a relief when they came to a halt.

Stearman felt an unpleasant thrill of suspense as he waited, blinking against the rough covering on his eyes, while his captors climbed down, boots scraping against the wagon bed, the wagon bouncing under their weight. He felt the horse blanket being removed, then hands reached for him, dragging him to the ground, pulling and jostling him roughly towards his destination.

He had been listening intently to a noise that had been getting louder all the time. Now he was sure that it was running water, a lot of running water, flowing fast and strongly. He could feel the chill of it from where he stood.

They took off his blindfold, ripping it cruelly from his head, almost taking his earlobe with it. He looked at what they had brought him to. It was a river, deep but not particularly wide, surging through a narrowing of the high riverbank. The water was rolling and twisting around rocks and boulders on its journey to what lay around the next bend in its course. Stearman could hear what it was and he could see vapour rising and he knew that it must be a cataract, a drop in the river of about twenty feet or so.

The four men jostled Stearman toward the riverbank. Flooding at various times in the river's history had cut away the bank, making it sheer, a short drop but a lethal one into the torrent of rushing water. Stearman dug in his heels and leaned away from his fate but refused to plead with them. He knew he would drown with his hands and ankles bound. He only hoped that he might be struck unconscious first. But even as he reviewed this fate he felt a jerk at his wrists and the rope was cut. The same was done to the tie around his ankles, though the men continued to hold him in an iron grip.

'This won't kill you. But it might make you think twice about coming poking around our town again,' one of the men said, close to his ear, and Stearman recognized the voice. He had spoken to this man at some point today. But still he clung to the belief that Parry was behind his kidnap.

'Tell Major Parry he's made his last mistake,' he replied, twisting his head to look at the big man who had spoken to him. He saw the four men look at each other, then with a shrug the one who had warned him gave Stearman a shove, a hand on his back and a boot against the back of his knees sending Stearman into the river head first.

CHAPTER 17

The river was a living thing, muscular and powerful, twisting and flexing as it carried Stearman along in its sinews, crushing him in its icy embrace, dragging him along the gritty riverbed until his lungs were like to burst, then casually freeing him to breathe again. He didn't struggle against the force of it. It was futile to fight against the might of thousands of gallons of thundering water, carrying him along like a giant that doesn't know its own strength. He spun and tumbled with no more resistance than a leaf, borne towards the roaring cataract, aware of its approach but helpless to save himself. With a last desperate gulp of air, he went over the waterfall and dropped into the maelstrom below, a boiling cauldron of icy water, agitated into foam and colder than anything Stearman had ever experienced. The water pulled him under and pinned him hard against sharp rock, then playfully turned him over and over and battered him with a series of vicious blows before releasing him into the mainstream again.

The river gentled here and Stearman felt the current carry him to the shallows, near the riverbank, casting him on to a tongue of gravel and sand a little way downstream.

He was utterly exhausted, beaten and half drowned,

103

unable to move for some time, but it was the cold that finally made Stearman get up on to his feet. He would not feel the results of his trip down the river until later, the alarming bruises, cuts and scrapes he had endured would make themselves painfully felt. Now he was numbed by the penetrating cold that was already sapping his will. He crawled, then stumbled up on to the bank, pausing only to pull off his boots and drain the river water out of them, while his whole body shook and juddered and his jaw clenched on chattering teeth.

Too exhausted to go back up river to find his coat, he began to walk back towards the town, following the track the wagon had taken, head ducked into the wind, wishing for respite from the biting cold. He had only gone a few hundred yards when an old one-horse wagon rattled up beside him. The driver was a man of advanced years with pale-blue eyes that watered in the cold wind, a hook of a nose and thin, hunched-up shoulders. He looked nearly as ramshackle as his rig. He studied Stearman with amused patience, noting his wet condition and the shuddering of his limbs with cold.

'You are in one sorry state, son,' he declared. 'You fall in that river?'

'No, sir, I had a little help.'

'Better jump on, then,' 'fore pneumonia sets in.'

'You going into town?'

'Road only goes but one way.'

Stearman was glad of the ride, especially as the substantial rear quarters of the big, slow horse shielded both of them from the wind a little. The old man never spoke another word except to tell him there was a blanket behind him he'd be welcome to use, if he wanted. His passenger was some distance away from town without a horse; he had obviously been in a river that was too cold to venture into in high summer, let alone late autumn, and he had cuts and bruises aplenty. He'd had a run-in with something or somebody that was bigger and uglier than he was, but it was none of the old man's business and he was just glad to be of help.

Stearman gratefully turned round and found an old army-issue blanket. He pulled it around himself, burying his chin in its rough woollen folds. He was surprised but was too tired to comment when the driver turned his rig off the main road on to a narrow, rutted side road which led to a smallholding.

The farmhouse was a good size and had been added to quite skilfully at least three times in its lifetime. It was well cared for, painted white, with its back to the mountains. It seemed colder to Stearman here than it had in Randolph. The mountains were closer, and that meant the winter was closer.

'Go on inside. I need to take care of Arabella,' the old man told him, and Stearman stiffly got down, still clutching the blanket around him. It took him a minute to realize that Arabella was the horse.

The front door opened directly on to a large, well-furnished living area, with a big fireplace and, more importantly, a big fire. The rich smell of burning wood, a wonderful, life-giving heat, curiously made Stearman shiver all the more. He had got as close to it as safety would allow when he heard a voice speaking from an adjoining room.

'Is that you, Dad? Did you bring Joe with you?' A small, dark, robustly built woman of thirty or so came into the room with a smile of welcome on her face. It slowly faded when she saw Stearman. But she expressed no fear, only mild surprise and curiosity.

'Where'd you come from?' she asked, but not unkindly.

'Sorry to trouble you, ma'am, but I had a . . . a little difficulty and your . . . the gentleman with the rig offered me a ride. My name's John Stearman.'

'Glad to meet you, Mr Stearman. Goodness, is that our old horse blanket you're wearing? Was it the river you had a little difficulty with?' she asked. Like the old man, she seemed to find his predicament amusing.

The front door opened and the man himself came in, stamping his feet as if he had been out in three feet of snow. He disposed of his hat and coat and came into the room, smiling at the woman.

'There you are, Maude. Found this young fella on the road, had a mite of difficulty down by the river; brought him back to get him warmed up and dried out.'

The woman nodded, as if it was only the right thing to do. She looked fondly at the older man and Stearman gauged that they were father and daughter.

'This young lady is my daughter Maude Garrett. Her husband Joe will be along directly. He went in to see Ben Stillman,' he said in an aside to his daughter, and she nodded.

'Is he going to walk back, Dad?'

'Guess he will. Now, while we're standing about talking, this young man is makin' a puddle on the rug.'

Maude laughed and looked down. True enough, there was a wet circle under Stearman's feet. She bustled away and was gone for ten minutes or so, during which time the man introduced himself as Bob Turner and gave Stearman a drink of home-made apple cider, which warmed him more than the fire had done but increased the feeling of weariness he had felt since battling the river.

Maude returned then and guided Stearman into her kitchen, a long, low-ceilinged room with a stone floor, a cooking range loaded with pots, all simmering and bubbling at various stages of readiness, and a big old scarred kitchen table, already set for supper. She took Stearman through this room and into another, a brick-lined room with a sink and a big copper for hot water. She had already filled a hip bath for him and put towels and soap on a chair beside it.

'Leave your clothes at the door, Mr Stearman,' she said over her shoulder. She returned to her kitchen, leaving him to fumble with buttons that had mysteriously swollen and refused to pass through the buttonholes, a belt buckle that resisted all his efforts to loosen it and boots that he didn't have the energy to shuck. His hands were so cold and shook so much he was as helpless as a new-born infant. Then, as if he had read Stearman's mind, Bob Turner came into the washhouse and wordlessly set about helping him, without any fuss, just a murmured, 'All right, son,' as Stearman was stripped of all his wet clothes. Turner didn't find the ugly bruising on Stearman's body quite so funny now. He waited just to make sure Stearman got safely into the big tub of warm water, then left him to sink down into its reviving heat. With his head tilted on a towel over the edge of the zinc bath he drifted into an exhausted sleep.

He emerged half an hour later, warm at last, and clean of the mud and weed and grit of the river, dressed in someone else's work shirt and pants. Stearman had no complaint about them being a little too short and too wide. They were clean and they were dry. In the big kitchen the Turner family were seated for supper: two young men, dark like their sister Maude, another fair-haired, bearded man, Maude's husband Joe Garrett; and a little girl of about six or seven, with long blonde hair and a turned-up nose, who was sitting close to Bob Turner. She was explaining the complexities of a story she had read in her school book, while Turner nodded and murmured encouragement as he buttered a thick slice of bread for her.

When Stearman came into the room, they all looked up with smiling, friendly curiosity. One by one, they got up to introduce themselves. The two brothers were Robert and Bill, and the little girl was Cathy.

'Come and sit down, Mr Stearman. Have a little supper with us. You were so long your bath must have grown cold,' Maude observed, putting a plate of roast chicken in front of him and indicating the various bowls of vegetables, the bread plate and sauce boat. One of the brothers poured him a glass of milk, though there was a pitcher of beer on the table too.

'This is very kind,' he said quietly, with a nod to his host.

'We're just nosy, want to know how you came to fall in the river,' the other brother said and there was good-natured laughter.

'I had a disagreement with somebody who isn't man enough to settle the matter face to face,' Stearman replied, for the first time speaking a little bitterly. He was instantly sorry for it when he saw that the others didn't know how to respond, and for a time there was an awkward silence, till the youngest member of the group broke the ice.

'Is that my daddy's shirt you're wearing, Mr Stearman? 'Cause if it is, you can most probably keep it. My mamma said it was only fit for a dishrag.' She turned for confirmation first to her poker-faced grandfather, then to her busily eating father and uncles, and lastly looked to her horrified mother. 'Didn't you, Mamma?'

The Turners had a spare bedroom at the top of the house for visiting family, with a big bed, comfortable in a lumpy sort of way. Maude aired and warmed it thoroughly with a couple of stone hot-water bottles before Stearman sank gratefully into it that night. He was stuffed with roast chicken and cherry cobbler, now he lay snug beneath a patchwork quilt that smelt of lavender.

At dinner tonight he had been fed and entertained, plied with mild liquor and given the best chair by the fire afterwards. The two younger men had wanted to talk about the war, though Maude's husband Joe, who had seen action at Antietam and both battles at Bull Run, exchanged a dark, knowing look with him. Cathy wanted to tell him the story from her school book and wheedled herself on to his knee, mainly so that she could artlessly question him about his home and family. Stearman spun a story of air and nonsense and soon had her in the palm of his hand, giggling and growing noisier by the minute until Maude declared it to be long past bedtime. But Cathy refused to go until she had shown Stearman her greatest treasure, which was a mahogany box filled with odds and ends of great value and sentimentality to Cathy. Stearman thought that its original use might have been as a tea caddy, for his mother had owned one just like it. It was locked and Cathy produced a tiny key which, she whispered to him, was kept in a secret place. She showed him the coins and shells and trinkets she had either gathered or been given during her short life. Stearman begged to add to her collection by giving her a silver dollar that he had carried as a good luck piece for many years. It had been given to him as a boy by his grandfather. This gift delighted her far beyond its worth. As he watched her turn the tiny key, a fleeting memory tried to surface. He frowned, trying to remember what it was: the same slightly nagging thought that bothered him after his words with Harry and Jumper, but, just as then, he couldn't pin it down.

Later that night, as the comforting fire died, Turner

asked Stearman what had brought him to Dansing. Stearman explained about Hobie and how he had been unable to find him. Turner had nodded and turned his gaze on the settling embers of the fire.

'The Hobarts? Oh, that was real sad. They all died,' he said. 'Diphtheria.'

As he lay snug in the folds of clean linen, his body aching but not intolerably so, Stearman thought about Hobie, about a life that had never had time to amount to anything, cut short by the same foul disease that had decimated his own family. He owed that young man so much, and he was sorry now that he had not sought him out sooner to thank him.

But as he started to slip into a much-needed sleep, it was Cathy's treasure box that came into his mind, and the little key that she kept in a secret place. At last, his eyes closed and his breathing evened, he remembered.

CHAPTER 18

Helen Knight had a long, homely face and prominent collar and wrist bones. She was dressed fashionably in a mauve morning gown and wore expensive earrings that glinted and caught the light when she moved her head. Everything about her spoke of wealth, as did her home: a large, elaborate house in the best quarter of the town of Lydia. It was tastefully furnished, with every comfort. For an instant Stearman thought of Lisbeth in her tiny, unheated garret room, before he refocused on his hostess. She had ordered coffee to be served with little lemon sponge cakes, served by Betsy Ross's replacement, an Irish girl who looked uncomfortable in her stiff cambric dress and apron. Stearman had eaten three of the cakes before he stopped himself with an apologetic smile, to which Mrs Knight merely smiled, pleased that he liked them. He hadn't eaten since, early that morning, he'd taken breakfast with the adults of the Turner household, before Turner himself drove him to the railroad station. They'd parted as friends, Stearman's thanks shrugged off, his hand firmly shaken before the old man turned and reached behind him for something Stearman hadn't expected to see again, his coat, retrieved this morning from the riverbank by one of Turner's boys. Then, with a parting wave, he was gone, to drive Arabella homewards.

Now here he was in Lydia, in the home of Betsy Ross's last employer, with one or two questions.

'She was a very sweet girl, hard-working and honest. My two girls adored her,' Helen Knight told him as she poured her second cup of coffee, which she drank black and unsweetened. 'When she didn't come home we didn't know what to think. At first we decided she must be ill and had stayed over with her cousin, but after a few days with no word from her we knew it must be more than that. Then her cousin wired us to ask if she had come home, and we knew something was amiss. My husband went to Randolph himself to make enquiries.'

'Did she ever mention that she had a special friend or a sweetheart in Randolph?'

'No; at least, she never spoke of anyone to me. I've questioned Mrs Craig, our cook, but Betsy never confided in her if there was someone.'

Stearman put his cup down carefully on the low table between them, resisted the last lemon cake and cleared his throat to make his next suggestion.

'Have you gone through her things to see if she had any correspondence that might tell you if she planned to meet someone in Randolph?'

'Yes,' Mrs Knight said, looking unhappy about it. She fidgeted with the lace edging of her cuffs and looked anxiously at Stearman. 'My husband looked through the little desk in her room but there were only old letters from family and a girl she knew who moved to St Louis. There was nothing else that he could see.'

'Ma'am, would you have any objection to letting me have a look?' Stearman asked. Helen Knight looked at him doubtfully, then nodded and led the way to her room, because she knew, as Stearman knew, that Betsy probably wasn't coming back and was hardly likely to mind someone poking around in her things. The unspoken subtext which they both recognized was that she had come to grief somehow and what they needed to do now was find out what had happened to her.

The room was at the top of the house, which Stearman had expected. What he hadn't expected was to find a prettily furnished bedroom that could as easily have belonged to a member of the family. It was furnished with white-painted furniture, a comfortable armchair, a writing desk and chair and a good-sized bed. There were mirrors and pictures on the walls and good quality, heavy, pale-blue drapes hung by the single window. Stearman smiled as he looked around.

'I imagine she was very happy and comfortable here,' he said. Mrs Knight nodded and sighed.

'We thought she was.'

From the ground floor, a voice called up to her, an elderly female voice. She left the room, replying that she was on her way; she looked back at Stearman.

'My mother. She lives with us. Would you excuse me for a moment, Mr Stearman?' she asked but left without waiting for his reply.

Stearman didn't waste his opportunity and began searching the room, every shelf and closet and drawer, calmly and systematically, until he had run out of places to look. She didn't have that much anyway, so most of the drawers in the bureau were empty. Puzzled, he sank down on to the bed, sitting with his forearms resting on his thighs, trying to put himself into the mind of a nineteen-year-old female. It was the squeak of his boot on a loose board that led him to her hiding-place, beside and just underneath the bed. He knelt to prise it up with his clasp knife and found what he had been looking for. It was smaller than Cathy's treasure box and it fitted into Stearman's inside coat pocket with hardly a bulge: a white-painted box decorated with little glass beads and pieces of mirror glass. It was locked.

He met Mrs Knight on the stairs.

'You didn't find anything either?'

'I'm sorry, ma'am. But I promise you, if I hear any news of her I'll be in touch.'

He called next at the rooming-house where Tipper had lately boarded. It was close in kind to Mrs Joe's place in Randolph: a big old house, unpainted, badly weathered, with a constantly changing clientele. Except that this rooming-house was spotlessly clean and well-tended, lived-in but not neglected. The caretaker was Russian, a short and stocky man with close-cropped dark hair and deep-set brown eyes. Like the rooming-house, he was a little rubbed at the edges but neat and clean in appearance. He had anglicized his name from Galinsky to plain Galen. He invited Stearman into the cubbyhole that was his office and offered him a chair.

'How may I be of assistance?' he asked courteously.

'I believe you recently had a guest by the name of Tipper staying here. Is that correct?'

The caretaker took a little while to answer and at first Stearman thought he was being cautious, thinking over everything he would say before speaking, but as they conversed he realized that Galen was translating everything back into Russian in his head.

'He is regular. He leaves clothes, and other things here, and then travels with his little bag, to show samples.'

'What kind of samples?'

'Liquor, in little bottles. But it is strange, for he left a few days ago and has not returned. Usually he tells me if he is going away. He returned early – very early – one morning, but left again shortly after. I have not seen him since then.'

'Is he prompt at paying his rent?'

Brown lingered over the word 'prompt' before giving a little shrug.

'Sometimes, sometimes not. He likes to play the games, the cards, you know. But he always squares with me eventually. He went to a regular card game in Randolph every other Friday but he lost a lot of money last time. He said to me, "Alex, I am rooked," but he laughed and said he would come about.'

'Mr Tipper won't be coming back for some time, I'm afraid. He's landed himself in a bit of trouble.'

'What has he done?'

'He killed a man in Randolph and he might be involved in a young woman's disappearance.'

The caretaker looked surprised at this. 'You say my Mr Tipper did this thing?'

'I'm afraid so, sir.'

'That he might have been involved with a girl?'

'Well, he forced his attentions on a young woman on a train and she subsequently disappeared.'

The caretaker stared at Stearman, then shook his head as if completely baffled.

'This is not the Tipper I know,' he said with a rueful smile.

'In what way?'

The caretaker hesitated, not wishing to cause his tenant any further trouble, but he had to set the record straight, if Tipper was being wrongly accused.

'His preference in the past has not been for girls,' Galen said with a little gesture of one shoulder and one hand. 'If you see what I mean?'

'Other men?'

'Boys, the younger the better. He almost lost his place here because of it. I had to speak to him on one occasion, when his young friend was making so much noise. Usually he was very discreet. But not girls. I think there may be some mistake there.'

'Mr Galen, I think you might just have saved Mr Tipper from the hangman.'

CHAPTER 19

For all its surface glitter, mirrors, lamps, a handsome teak bar with a brass footrail and clean glasses, Miller's bar on Weston Street was just that, a bar, with a thick haze of cigar smoke and the smell of liquor and of men in company together. There were no women on the premises and the owner employed two well-dressed bouncers to keep order, which they did to good effect. There were seldom any brawls and never any gunplay in Miller's.

Stearman walked in that night a little after seven and ordered a whiskey at the bar. When it came he drank it down and paid for another. When he had this in his hand, he turned to scan the room until he found what he was looking for.

Jack Parry was sitting with three other men, wearing an expensive coat and smoking an expensive cigar. He had a bottle of bourbon on the table and had been filling up everyone's glass, getting these three important townspeople on side for some reason of his own. He was flattering and cajoling them by turns, joking and, with apparent sincerity, listening to them. A born politician, he had his eye on the governor's mansion, and the senate someday, but for now he had to make himself amenable to anybody who could give him a leg-up.

It was the sudden silence of these men that alerted him to the man who had come to stand by his table uninvited. Parry looked up into Stearman's face and the foolish smile of bonhomie died on his lips.

'I hope Sergeant Parry is keeping you all entertained,' Stearman said to the questioning faces of the men around the green baize table. The three men who shared Parry's liquor that night were perhaps not so enamoured of the councilman as he thought they were, and at least two of them – Mark Standen, a newspaperman, and Enoch Wheatley, the owner of the town's biggest general store – thought a good deal more of John Stearman than they did of Parry and his flash clothes and free drinks. Standen, florid and handsome, with full side whiskers and shrewd brown eyes, leaned back in his chair with his glass held at chest height, a slight smile on his face. He observed that Stearman was armed, with a revolver tucked into his belt. His topcoat concealed the weapon but wasn't buttoned.

'I think you mean Major Parry,' the third man, Bob Steep, said, glancing interestedly at Parry, then back again at the newcomer, whom he didn't know. Steep was a lawyer and no drinker, but he had been invited tonight to hear some proposition of Parry's and he, like many another, didn't like to get on the wrong side of him.

'Beg your pardon. I must be mistaken,' Stearman said, his voice flat.

'I'm busy here, Stearman,' Parry said in the tone of someone humouring an inferior. 'Don't you have a coffin somewhere you need to be making?' He smirked at his own badinage.

'Don't you have any Rebels that need hanging?' Stearman

asked in the same tone. Parry slowly put his glass down and looked around as if he no longer recognized his surroundings.

'What did you say?'

As he looked at the faces ranged around the barroom table, Stearman wondered if he had made a mistake in coming here straight from the train. He had felt the effects of the river today, his bruised body was hurting very badly in places and his temper was only just held in check. The source of his trouble sat nursing his drink, in his rich clothes and fine linen, and Stearman wanted to hurt him and expose him as a fraud and a liar. But he saw that this head-on approach was not going to work with Parry.

'I'd like a word,' he said in a neutral tone.

'Make an appointment.' Parry dismissed him and turned his body away slightly.

'Well, I don't mind if these gentlemen hear our business, if you don't,' Stearman said reasonably and he watched as Parry thought about what that business might be.

For a minute he looked as if he might just be stupid and arrogant enough to call Stearman's bluff, and then his own overweening ambition overrode his hair-trigger temper and he turned slowly back to face Stearman, put his glass down and stood up. He adjusted his vest and tie and pushed the bottle into the middle of the table.

'Please help yourselves, gentlemen. This won't take long,' he said pleasantly, but his neck was red with choler and his jaw was clenched as he walked out of the bar with Stearman behind him. On the boardwalk outside Parry thrust his hands into his pants pockets and turned to face his visitor.

'I haven't got all night,' he said with a sigh.

'I would have thought you would be grateful I didn't put an end to your pathetic little career in there.'

'What could you possibly do to hurt me? You're practically nothing in this town. And unless you stop this harassment, you're going to lose what little you do have.'

'Such as my job and my home?'

Parry leaned a hip on the railing that edged the boardwalk, and gave Stearman a bland look.

'Don't know what you're referring to.'

'What about sending half a dozen men to try to kill me?' Stearman asked, and this time Parry looked straight at him, a slight frown between his eyes.

'I didn't send . . .' Stearman had had enough. His arm shot out and Parry took the full impact of the big bunched fist on his chin. His legs flew up in the air as he tipped over the railing and landed in the road. Stearman circled the railing, hauled him upright and dragged him dazed and bleeding into the alley at the side of the saloon. He pinned him against the wall by jerking his coat down over his upper arms. He caught his full attention by pressing the barrel of his revolver against Parry's ear.

'Now listen to me. I want to know what happened to Betsy Ross and I want to know why you've been trying to make my life difficult. I think they're both for one and the same reason, but I'm waiting to hear you tell me all about it.'

Parry's head was still spinning from the first blow. He felt the gun barrel against his temple and saw the light in Stearman's eyes. He swallowed several times, his usually agile brain failing to come up with any easy solution to his predicament.

'I never sent anybody after you,' he protested, but Stearman looked unconvinced. 'I don't know who did that to you but it wasn't me, I swear it.'

'What about the girl?'

'Here we go with this again. I'm telling you, I don't know

anything about her.'

'Then why did you lose me my room and my job? The only connection I've ever had with you, apart from the ferry, is Betsy Ross. You're a liar. You've lied about your army rank, lied to everybody in this town about what you and your friends did after the war, and you're lying now about the girl.'

'Prove it,' Parry defied him, with the fanatic light in his eye of someone who believes he has become too powerful to be answerable to the likes of one pitiful coffin-maker.

Stearman lowered his weapon and stepped back, allowing Parry to shrug himself back into his coat and wipe the blood from his mouth. They were standing close to a rain butt and he scooped some of the water to splash in his face, then pulled out a clean handkerchief to mop his chin. His eyes glittered with malicious good humour, with the knowledge that he had the better of Stearman, that he would always win out over men like him.

Stearman regarded him thoughtfully, wondering how any man could be so arrogant and self-deluding. He reached into his inner coat pocket and removed the little bundle of letters that Betsy Ross had treasured and kept hidden in her room, tied in a pink ribbon and thumbed and read over and over till she knew them by heart. The moment he took them out Parry knew what they were. His jaw tightened and he swore, calling the girl a filthy name.

'This proof enough?' Stearman asked.

'It's proof I wrote to her. What of it?' Parry blustered, the colour rising from his neck into his face.

'It's a little bit more than that, Councillor. You were lovers. These letters spell it out. You were the lover of a young girl who worked for you, who should have been under your protection. What happened? Why did she move to Lydia?'

'My wife got wind of it. She sent the kid packing. As far as I was concerned, that was the end of it.'

He massaged the back of his neck and stared at the ground, repeating to himself the vow he had made then: never to get involved with household staff again. But oh, she'd been hard to resist, especially when she was naked in her little narrow servant's bed, legs wide, waiting for him to cover her.

Quietly he said, 'She wrote to say she wanted to meet me; she had something important to tell me. I ignored it, didn't answer the letter, so she wrote again. This time she told me she was pregnant and she was coming to see me whether I wanted her to or not. But I didn't get the letter until after she went missing. I never saw her that night, I swear it. We had people in for dinner that night and I never left the house.'

Stearman was silent, but thoughtful rather than disbelieving.

'I don't know where she is,' Parry said. Stearman got the impression that this whole business had been an annoyance to him more than anything else, that the young girl he had so casually ruined had become a tiresome complication and an obstacle on his journey up the greasy pole.

'I'd say you've got a pretty powerful reason for getting rid of her,' he stated. Parry opened his mouth to utter a denial, but saw the futility of doing so.

'You have to believe me, Stearman, I didn't hurt her. I couldn't hurt that girl. I was actually pretty fond of her,' he whined and Stearman wanted to hit him again, knock him into the middle of next week in fact. But he believed him, at least about his having a cast-iron alibi. But Parry was involved in Betsy's disappearance somehow, he was equally sure of that.

'Is this the way you mean to get to the top, Parry? Somebody happens to be in your way and you just go straight over them.'

'What other way is there?' Parry asked. He had recovered his composure a little, and stood with legs slightly apart, putting his disordered clothing to rights with the air of a man looking in his own dressing-room mirror. 'Nice folks don't make it to the White House.'

'The White House?' Stearman asked incredulously, eyebrows raised, arms folded. 'You seriously think you're going to make it to Washington?' It was a sobering thought.

'I believe I may do just that,' Parry said with quiet confidence. Stearman almost admired his self-belief, no matter how misguided. But the thought of this arrogant little toad reaching the senate was too unpleasant to swallow. Stearman stepped up close to him again and asked him, 'Have you forgotten Constarry Crossing?'

'What?' It took a while but Parry finally remembered. Stearman had mentioned the ferry just now and called him sergeant earlier. And he had spoken of hanging a Rebel.

'Don't you remember me, Councilman? I was at the ferry. I saw what you and your friends did.'

'How were you. . .?'

Stearman gripped Parry's arm and pushed back his coat and shirtsleeve, revealing a small blue scar like a tiny knot under the skin.

'I did this,' he said softly. 'Just after you cut down young Hobie.'

Parry stared at him trying to recall. He dimly remembered the army major who had tried to stop the proceedings, but the details weren't clear.

'And what did you see exactly? Some soldiers hanging a Rebel? Nobody will turn a hair if they hear we did that.'

'You're right. I didn't see what you did inside the ferry house. Hobie told me, after he saved my life when you and your friends tried to kill me.'

'And where is Hobie now? It's your word against mine, Stearman, and in case you hadn't noticed, I'm a man of some consequence in this town. You're no threat to me. I wonder why I ever thought you were.' Parry twisted his arm free to pull his sleeve down again. If Stearman was the worst his chequered past could throw up, then his future was in no danger. He made a little heel turn as if to go but was stopped by Stearman's next words.

'Not me, Sergeant, but maybe somebody else.'

'What does that mean?'

'Someone's on the hunt, Parry, picking off all the men at the ferry. Hunter, the Rawl brothers and Randall Anderson. They're all dead, all but you and your colonel. Even Hobie is dead. Maybe somebody else wants to protect his career. Maybe somebody lost a mother or sister or daughter to you and the others and doesn't want to leave it alone.'

Parry knew about two of the deaths, but in his arrogance he believed they could easily be explained. Now, for the first time, he faced the idea that he was one of a select few remaining witnesses to some grisly events in the past and his usual way of dealing with problems, with brute force, bluster, cruelty and coercion wouldn't help if there was someone stalking him. He looked at Stearman and realized that while he had been hounding him, all the time a greater danger existed.

'You think you can strong-arm your way to the White House, riding roughshod over anybody that gets in your way, and that pregnant housemaids and people like me who know what you were and what you really did in the war are going to just go away, Councilman?' Stearman laughed harshly and returned the incriminating letters to his coat pocket. 'I guess we'll have to see about that. You take care now,' Stearman cautioned. He turned round and walked away, leaving Councilman Parry standing alone in the shadows.

CHAPTER 20

Doc Moss was out when Stearman looked in at the sheriff's office. A lone deputy sat at the desk, a young fellow whom Stearman knew as Beau. He was reading the paper and drinking coffee.

'Something I can help you with, Mr Stearman?' he asked.

'Doc's gone home for the night.'

'I'd like to have a word with Tipper.'

Beau's face remained affable. He had a clear-skinned youthfulness that made him look about eighteen, but his eyes were lawman's eyes and were suddenly wary.

'What about?'

'I'm hoping he might have some information that will be of help to the sheriff. I won't need but a minute.'

Beau squinted and chewed the inside of his mouth. Doc had left him in charge, which he didn't do all that often, and he was mindful of his responsibilities. But from what the sheriff had said, Stearman was all right.

'Have to ask you to leave any weapons here on the desk, if you have any,' he said reasonably. Stearman obliged, placing his Colt revolver down on the desk top. He held out his arms to indicate that Beau could search if he wanted. But the deputy just reached for the keys in the drawer and led

126

CONSTARRY CROSSING

the way to the back area, which held four cells, two large and two small. Tipper was in one of the small ones, stretched out on his bunk with his arms behind his head. Beau hung around for a minute, awkwardly, not sure if he should insist on staying or not but seeing that Stearman wanted him to go, he returned to the front office. On the cot Tipper stirred and sat up. He shuffled to his feet and came to stand at the bars, looking with reluctant interest at Stearman.

'How are you doing, Tipper?'

'All right, I guess. The food's OK and they make a decent cup of coffee, but the beds are nothing to write home about.'

'Do you mind if I ask you a question?' Stearman stepped nearer to the bars, looking closely at Tipper. He looked much cleaner than before, close shaved and his hair neatly trimmed. His clothes had been washed too and he presented an altogether less menacing picture than he had on the train or when they arrested him. In answer to Stearman's question he shrugged.

'What do you want to know?'

'On the train, that was the first time you ever did anything like that, wasn't it.'

Tipper weighed up Stearman's words, tracing a mark on the floor with his toe.

'Yes, sir, it was. I'm not proud of it.'

'Who asked you to do it?'

Tipper looked surprised. He scratched his chin and frowned, wondering where this was leading, wondering if it was going to get him deeper into trouble.

'What makes you think anybody asked me?'

Stearman let the silence lengthen, his head tilted, a questioning, expectant look on his face.

'Because I spoke to your landlord, that's why.'

After a while Tipper finally got the idea. He flushed and burned Stearman a look.

'Well, I ain't gonna stand up in court and tell everybody what I am.'

'Maybe you won't need to.'

Stearman took the handbill that he had seen outside the sheriff's office in Dansing from his coat pocket. It was hand-written, a desperate plea from the family of a girl who had gone missing on the day of Tipper's arrest. He passed it through the bars.

'You know that the girl you spoke to is missing? Well, this girl here is missing too.'

Tipper read the handbill over and over but he didn't get it. He looked up, puzzled, and shook his head.

'What?'

'Read it one more time,' Stearman encouraged, a patient schoolmaster to his least apt pupil. Tipper gave an exaggerated sigh and peered down at the paper. Then finally a light dawned in his eyes.

'I see it. This girl went missing when I was in here, right? So if you was to show this to the sheriff, he'd know I didn't have anything to do with any other girls going missing?'

'Could be,' Stearman shrugged. 'If he thought they were connected. But Doc Moss is a by-the-book kind of man. He'll want more proof than this. I think I can get that proof, if you talk to me.'

'Sure, but it doesn't help with that Anderson fella. They only need to hang me once.'

He passed the handbill back through the bars, but didn't move away. He looked expectantly, even hopefully at Stearman.

'If you tell me what I need to know, I'll speak up for you. You only came for your bag. You weren't expecting

Anderson to be waiting for you with a gun. You acted in simple self-defence. I'm not saying you won't do some jail time, but better that than a rope.'

It was a lifeline. Tipper grabbed it like a drowning man, pressing his thin face to the bars of his cell.

'It was an old buddy of mine. I owed him some money from a poker game. Said he knew the girl, wanted to stop her from running off with somebody. He said if I gave her a good scare she would likely go back home. So that's what I did.'

'Who? Who told you to give her a good scare, Tipper? Tell me and I'll do everything I can to help you.'

CHAPTER 21

In the outer office, Beau was deep in conversation with two other deputies and Doc Moss. Stearman felt a twinge of unease when he saw the expression on Doc's face. It was the look of a father who has been cruelly disappointed by a favourite child.

'I was just on my way to see you,' Stearman said to Doc Moss, but with a glance at the two deputies, large, capable-looking men, related to one another but not looking much alike. They were the sheriff's best two.

'You carrying, John?' the sheriff asked and Stearman felt a cold dread in his stomach. He stared into Doc's eyes for a clue.

'He already gave me his weapon, Doc,' Beau said.

Stearman wondered if this was about Jack Parry, about that little roughing-up he'd given him tonight. He was invited to sit in front of the desk, with the three deputies taking up positions on the other side of the room. Stearman didn't think he'd ever seen three deputies all together at once in all the time he'd lived in Randolph. Doc Moss sat down a little wearily behind his desk.

'Make a pot of coffee, would you, Beau?' he asked the youngest deputy, then he turned his attention to Stearman.

130

'John, can you tell me where you were at about eight o'clock tonight?'

Stearman strove for patience, fighting down a queer feeling of panic inside him. Something bad had happened tonight. He was in the frame for it and Doc Moss seemed to think he belonged there.

'I was in here talking to Tipper. What happened at eight o'clock?'

'Jack Parry was murdered.'

An ominous silence fell on the little group. The old clock on the wall ticked heavily and the water on the boil on the stove began to bubble under the pot lid. Beau turned his attentions to this and one of the others cleared his throat, while Stearman waited.

'You had words with him earlier tonight, that right, John?'

'I can hardly deny it. Half of Randolph was in Miller's at the time.'

'What about?'

'I didn't kill him, Doc,' Stearman stated flatly.

'Please, just let us get through with these questions for now.'

'You know why. He cost me my job and my room at Mrs Joe's. And yesterday I took a trip to try to find Hobie and some of Parry's men attacked me. I was damn lucky to walk away from that one, so yes, I had a few choice words with Councilman Parry. But when I left him he wasn't suffering from anything but a split lip. So, how did he die?'

'Stabbed in the back. He crawled into the middle of the street and died there. Couple of witnesses say they saw you hit him and then drag him into the alley about ten, fifteen minutes before that.'

'Funny no one came rushing to his rescue,' Stearman said as Beau put a cup of coffee on the desk in front of him and passed another across to Doc Moss.

'No one would spit on him if he was on fire,' Beau said and Doc Moss lowered his brows in the young deputy's direction.

'Thank you, Beau. Why don't you and Mel and Frank take a walk while I talk to John?'

'Yes, sir,' Beau said meekly and the three men reluctantly left the office.

'Did you find Hobie?' Moss asked when they were gone. Stearman shook his head and drank his coffee.

'They had an outbreak of diphtheria a while ago. I was told he died, him and all his family.'

'So that just leaves Colonel Bell and you,' the sheriff said.

'Either Bell's been on a killing spree or the whole thing has nothing to do with what happened at that ferry.'

'That's my belief, Doc. I think Colonel Bell is long gone and Parry and Anderson and the Rawls all had plenty of other enemies.'

'Well, still and all, I'm going to have to put you in one of my cells – for the night at least, John. The boys have got instructions to keep asking questions. They'll turn something up.'

Stearman got to his feet, draining the last of his coffee, while Doc reached for the keys to the cells. They stood regarding one another soberly for a moment or two, wondering what this was going to do to their friendship, when they both heard a cry, high and intense, the sound of someone in a lot of pain. The two men froze for a second before hurrying down the long narrow corridor at the rear of the building that housed the jail cells.

Tipper was lying on his bunk moaning softly. Doc reached him first and knelt beside him.

'Dear God in heaven,' he murmured, seeing the deep,

ragged wound high up in his chest on the right side. It was bleeding hard, a knife wound by the look of it, but it was as if the knife had been twisted in him, tearing the flesh. Tipper was grey and clammy with shock and rapid blood loss and his eyes were staring and bright with fear. Doc and Stearman both looked up at the high, narrow window. It was unglazed, but with a pair of shutters; both open and beyond them something moved, and they heard a thud and a grunt. Stearman turned and ran for the door.

On the cot Tipper was trying to speak. 'He said it'd be all right . . . he said. . . .'

'Who was it, Tipper? Did you see who it was?' Doc asked him urgently but he was slipping away, his grip on Doc's arm slackening. He stared up at the ceiling and died in that position, blood frothing from his nostrils and mouth as he breathed his last.

At the back of the building, where there was a narrow passageway hardly wide enough to admit an adult, two empty boxes had been placed under the narrow barred window slit in Tipper's cell. Stearman clambered up on to them and was able to look down into the cell where the prisoner lay dead now, staring up at him. There was blood on the window ledge and a bloody handprint on the bars.

'Somebody must have climbed up here and called to Tipper to come talk to him,' he said and Doc looked up at him, his face in shadow. 'Must've been somebody he knew.'

'Must've been,' Stearman agreed, his tone neutral, but he already knew who it was.

Doc returned to the office, just as Stearman walked in, holding his hands out palm up to show he had not seen anybody in the alley or outside. His face was grave as he cleaned blood from his hand with a towel Doc offered him.

'I wasn't expecting this,' Doc said, patting his breast

pocket absently.

'Neither was Tipper, I think.'

'Who the hell would want to kill him?' Doc questioned, sinking back into his chair, his hat shoved to the back of his head. 'Do you think it was the same fella who killed Parry?'

'As I'm about to be locked up for killing him, I think you mean me.'

'Shut up. I've enough on my plate without a wise-ass,' Doc grumped, fishing in a pocket for something he never found. Stearman took the flyer out of his pocket and gave it to Doc to read.

'I went to Lydia today and I found out Tipper owed somebody a lot of money,' Stearman said, neglecting to tell Doc Moss the most important thing he'd found out. 'You asked me what I wanted to speak to Tipper for. I wanted to show him that. I told him if that girl was connected to the Canvas Town girls and to Betsy, then he was in the clear. And I told him I'd speak up for him with regard to Randall Anderson. I said he was just trying to get his bag back, after all. He wasn't expecting the reception he got.'

Doc read the flyer and understood the significance right away, and if he thought Stearman was stretching a point about Anderson, he didn't show it. He smoothed a thumb over his moustache and carefully placed the flyer on the desk in front of him. He looked his age suddenly, the paper-thin skin at his temple was revealing a throbbing vein, his eyes were moist the way old men's eyes get sometimes, and his hand resting on the desk betrayed a slight tremor. His brain was still sharp but he was bone weary tonight and feeling every one of his years.

'Want to tell me what else is on your mind, John?' Stearman held back. He knew and he suspected enough to put most of the answers on a plate for the sheriff, but he needed to get this right. Before Stearman could answer, two of the deputies returned, looking pleased with themselves.

'Found us a witness says Parry was alive and well when Mr Stearman walked out of the alley. Says he went into the alley a little ways to ask Parry if he was all right and got told to go fuck himself.'

'Well, that's good enough for me,' Doc said, and he unlocked the desk drawer and withdrew Stearman's revolver. 'Glad we got that cleared up. No hard feelings, John?'

There was a serious undertone to Doc's voice that Stearman heard and understood perfectly. He held out his hand to show that he held no grudge.

'None at all, Doc.'

'I'll need a statement in the morning, son, get all this down on paper.'

'You know where to find me,' Stearman reminded the sheriff with a rueful smile.

'Could be there's one or two details you've forgot to tell me?' Doc wondered.

'I've got a feeling you're going to work it all out quite soon, Doc,' he said quietly, and he opened the door and was gone.

'That boy's holding out on me,' Doc said almost to himself, then he turned to his deputies.

Only Beau had noticed the bloody towel on the desk and the streak of blood on the sheriff's shirt collar. Doc Moss sighed and began to tell them about the fate of the late Mr Tipper.

135

CHAPTER 22

In the coffin workshop, a light glowed from a candle-lantern on the workbench beside the coffin Stearman had been working on. It flickered as he approached, casting wild shadows across the low ceiling and walls. Stearman looked around the workroom to see who was here, pivoting on his heel slowly, eyes probing the shadows before turning back to the workbench. The coffin had a lid on it, which hadn't been there yesterday morning, because he hadn't made a lid for it yet. It rested loose, not fixed, an oblong lid resting on the lozenge-shaped box. Stearman rested his hands on it and felt at once that the coffin had weight to it, that there was something inside. He moved the lid aside a little, then slid it back completely, pushed it over the edge of the bench and leaned over to look inside.

It was Lisbeth. His heart felt like it had been hit with a sledgehammer. Stearman's body jolted with the shock of it; his hands gripped the coffin edge and with a low moan of disbelief, he leaned closer.

'No! Oh, sweetheart, no,' he barely whispered, putting a hand on her shoulder. She was as pale and cold as marble, with an ugly bruise on her jaw. Her long plait was lying on her breast, still tied with one of the ribbons he had given her, and she was wearing her old, faded pink dress.

He had been too slow, hadn't worked it out quickly enough. He had been distracted by the whole business with Randall Anderson and Luther Rawl, had chased a two-year-old phantom when a real-life killer had been at work here in Randolph. Now this sweet girl had been killed, and Stearman turned away from her body to go and find her murderer, determined to succeed, even if it was the last thing he ever did.

He walked into a metal bar which swung in a short, brutal arc and dropped him like a felled tree. But for a few moments he was still conscious. He saw legs, four of them, one pair wearing dirty, mud-streaked boots, the other in shoes, black, highly polished. He heard two voices and ugly, brutish laughter, and the unmistakable sound of the lid being replaced on Lisbeth's coffin, before he felt himself sink down into a silence that wasn't entirely dark. Little sparks of light came and went in his head like fireflies; then even these went out and he was alone in the dark.

He woke sitting upright, tied to a chair, his head lolling to one side. A sickening throb of pain reminded him of the blow that had felled him. It was the kind of blow that usually kills. It had hit him on the left side of his head, splitting the skin just above his eyebrow. He had bled a river down one side of his face and into his shirt collar, leaving him feeling weak, light-headed and sick.

His first thought was for Lisbeth. What had they done to her before she died? What had she endured? A rage such as he hadn't felt since the first time he had lost men in the early battles of the war surged in him, scalding, unbearable, choking him, blinding him. He opened his eyes and came face to face with her killer.

It was Jumper, harmless, inebriated old Jumper, with his

warm, twinkling eyes and everybody's-favourite-uncle smile. He was sitting on a stool facing Stearman, his legs wide, hands on his thighs. He was completely sober for the first time Stearman could ever remember. Or perhaps he had never really been drunk. The iron bar he had used lay at his feet. He wasn't alone. Another man sat alongside him, one leg crossed over the other, hands in his pockets in a familiar manner. He wore no hat and his thick, luxuriant white hair fell in wings on either side of his temples.

'You always seem to be butting in to my affairs, John,' Harry Barclay chided him gently, 'First at the ferry you try to stop the lawful hanging of a Rebel prisoner, then you start poking around looking for missing young women. You've become much too much of a problem, m'boy. You have to be contained, for all our sakes. What say you, Jumper?'

'I'm afraid so, Colonel,' Jumper agreed.

'You're Colonel Bell?' Stearman asked.

'I have that honour. You never did see me at the ferry, did you, John? I came up behind you. And then I told young Hobie to dispose of you. It would appear he disobeyed me. I'd be interested to know how he did it.'

'He dug a hole, then filled it in again and put me in a root cellar till it was dark.'

'Resourceful lad. But his heart was never in our campaigns, was it, Jumper? He was inclined to be skittish.'

'We should never have taken him along, Colonel. I knew right off he was the wrong sort of man for us.'

'You weren't there,' Stearman said to Jumper, but it was the colonel who answered.

'Jumper was wounded the week before we reached the Constary River that day. We had to leave him behind for a spell.'

'And when you'd done with your looting and killing, you

came here?'

'I saw the way the wind was blowing. The war was over and the others were all of a mind to go home. This place belonged to a cousin of mine. He took me on as a partner, then obliged me by dying almost immediately. I saw its potential, you see, the convenience of half-empty graves and the relative isolation. Our work can get a little noisy. Things changed after the war, you know, John. Women started doing things they never did before. They got jobs men used to do, went out alone, they travelled on trains alone. That never used to happen. But as I said, we saw the potential.'

Stearman swallowed hot sickness, bitter as gall. He could scarcely bear to be in the same room as the two of them.

'You were getting close, weren't you, John?' Jumper said, leaning forwards with his forearms on his thighs. 'What was it tipped you off?'

Stearman struggled to remember; the crushing pain inside his head was almost past bearing.

'I had my suspicions but it was Tipper who gave me your name, just before you killed him. It was you, wasn't it, Jumper?'

'He would've talked if he had been in jail much longer. He could have caused me quite a bit of difficulty,' Jumper admitted with a casual shrug.

'And you took something out of your pocket the other day. I remembered what it was later on.'

Jumper emptied his pockets as he had done before, examining the string and the keys and buttons and coins. Then he smiled at the item John Stearman had noticed, a little brass key, the key to Betsy Ross's keepsake box. He picked it up and swung it back and forth with a grubby finger and thumb.

'The little Ross girl was wearing it on a chain around her

pretty neck. I clean forgot about it. Anything else?'

'A young girl's gone missing in Dansing. Did you take her? Did you kill her too?'

'No, sir.' Jumper wagged his head, keeping one eye squeezed shut, as if trying to remember. 'I don't recall any girl from Dansing.'

'Never went that far out. Too risky, Lydia, Cutter's Mill sometimes, but never Dansing,' Bell agreed with a brisk nod.

'How did you work it?' Stearman asked, looking from one to the other. 'On the train. One of you mauled the girls, the other stepped in to save them? Then you pretend to walk them home, carry their bags, then what?'

'Oh, we rang the changes on that. We only took a few from the train. All the others came from Canvas Town. They didn't have family mostly, or they were girls of low morals. Nobody missed them. Sometimes we'd coax them out here on some pretext, or we'd get them into Jumper's rooms. Jumper pushing a handcart with a coffin on it never excited any curiosity.'

'What part did Councilman Parry play in it all?'

'He played no part as it happens. Too concerned with his precious career, and anyway, he said he was done with the killing when the war finished. For him it was just all about fighting the war, being a soldier. That's why he gave himself a nice big fat promotion when it was all over,' the colonel said, and he and Jumper fell to laughing about that: Jack Parry and his vanity.

'But you killed the girl, Betsy. She was on her way to meet him that night.'

'Yes, she was supposed to meet our councilman that night. She'd written to ask for a meeting, to tell him she was expecting his baby. He was at his wits' end, so I asked him if he wanted me to take care of her for him. He hummed and hawed a bit, then agreed it might be for the best.'

'Yeah, *his* best,' Jumper sneered.

'You nearly ruined all our plans, coming so gallantly to her aid. Poor Tipper wasn't expecting to be put off the train. When she came back after getting rid of you I took care of her. Parry made sure he had a solid alibi that night, but when you started asking questions, he got spooked, told me to fire you, tried every which way to get rid of you.'

'Was he becoming a liability too? Which one of you killed him?'

They looked at one another. Jumper shook his head and shrugged.

'We didn't hear about that. Murdered? When?'

'Stabbed in the back tonight, just outside Miller's bar.'

'He wasn't without his enemies, it has to be said, but we didn't kill him,' Colonel Bell said.

'Shame he never made governor. He had his heart set on it,' Jumper added with a grin. 'No one else is in on this with us. Except when I asked Tipper to rough up the girl on the train because I'd hurt my shoulder. He didn't suspect a thing. He owed me and said he'd do it if I'd square the debt and give him a couple of bottles for his trouble. If you hadn't taken the colonel's bag, he would have gone back to Lydia none the wiser.'

'It was you,' Stearman said with a flash of insight, turning to look at the colonel. 'You got on the train at the water stop. I didn't recognize you. You were supposed to save the girl from Tipper; then what?'

'Do what we always did. Pretend I was a sweet old codger, slightly infirm and absent-minded and try to persuade her to come along with me. Amazing how gullible young women are, how trusting. They always fell for it. I waited at the station till she came back after you'd escorted her to the hotel. I said I would wait with her till Parry came, in the station waiting room,' the colonel explained. 'She never saw it coming. Had to take care of the whole thing m'self, though, what with Jumper being *hors de combat*. Got her back here all right, though. Had a nice snug place all ready for her. When Jumper's arm was better we buried her.'

In the silence that followed these stark revelations, the flame from the single candle danced and dipped in the draught. Stearman wondered what had caused the soft rush of air, but he didn't look around. Bell took his hands out of his pockets and massaged them together, while his eyes drifted about the orderly workroom.

'I've been killing girls since I was fifteen,' he said conversationally, giving the words no special import. 'Came into my own in the war. Lots of opportunities for men like us. But I think our time here may be just about over. What say you, Jumper?'

'Up to you, sir,' Jumper deferred, amiable to the last.

'And what about Lisbeth?' Stearman asked, trying to hold himself steady.

'Something upset her at Mrs Joe's. She came here looking for you and it just seemed too good an opportunity to miss,' Jumper supplied.

'Besides which, I've had my eye on her for some time. All that lovely hair and quite a womanly body under that old dress, despite her being so very young,' the colonel added, as if he were discussing some abstract academic problem.

Stearman and the chair he was tied to hurtled towards Bell like a missile, head first, with a roar of pure rage, barrelling into the colonel and slamming him into the floor. Stearman felt his head connect with bone, heard a satisfying crunch and felt the warm gush of the colonel's blood. Jumper hauled him off, dragging him to one side, raining blows on his head and body with fists, kicking him and bringing down a storm of profanity on him at the same time. He was on the point of delivering a killer blow with the iron bar which he had picked up, his face three different shades of purple with rage, when what seemed like a big yellow dog leapt on him, bringing him down on the floor with a great thud and a cloud of wood dust.

At least, that was the way it seemed to Stearman, half-conscious on the floor, still tied to the chair. But as the two shapes wrestled, he realized that the yellow dog was a man in a buckskin coat, with fair hair and big, powerful fists. He was pounding on the older man relentlessly till it was over, and the victor sitting astride Jumper, his right arm raised, his fist ready to drive down once more, but Jumper was insensible, maybe even dead; his attacker didn't care which. He stepped clear of the body and knelt beside Stearman to untie him.

'Are you all right, sir?' he asked, and Stearman realized it was Hobie, two years older, a bigger and stronger Hobie. He was unable to answer him at first, due to the beating he'd taken and the blow to the head earlier. The room tilted as if he was on the deck of a sailing ship when Hobie heaved him to his feet.

'Where did you come from?' he managed to get out.

'Came to find out if you were all right, Major,' Hobie said, looking uncomfortable, 'on account of how my friends nearly drowned you. I'm real sorry about that, sir.'

Stearman could only stare at the younger man, too dazed to comprehend.

'I heard about Phil Hunter and the Rawls, so I told all my friends that if somebody came into town looking for me, to say they didn't know where to find me. But I didn't think they'd do that to you.'

Stearman shook his head and felt as if he were capsizing.

He gripped Hobie's arm to stay upright.

'It was your friends that dumped me in the river?'

'Yes, sir. I found out about it next day and tried to find you.'

'That's quite a bit of loyalty you've got back there, Hobie.'

'Yes, sir, they're a decent bunch, most of the time.'

'Well, I can't say I enjoyed the experience very much but there was no real harm done. Well, not much. Some people took care of me. Bill Turner and his family.'

'They're good people, sir. Looked after me for a while when my folks died.'

Stearman lurched again. His head felt like it would never be right again.

'Colonel Bell's gone, sir.'

Stearman looked and saw the pool of blood on the ground and the trail of it leading to the door. He stepped clear of Hobie's encircling arm and, unsteadily, started to follow.

'Tie him up,' he instructed, pointing to Jumper. At the door, he took a couple of big breaths and braced a shoulder against the door jamb, searching for a sign of the colonel.

CHAPTER 23

He had gone into the cemetery. Stearman caught up with him by the east wall, the oldest part of the graveyard, where there was a rusting gate, long disused and locked, but the colonel had not intended to leave by the gate. He had come for his bag, which had been left by the grave Jumper had dug for Lisbeth. The colonel was crouched by the lip of the grave, looking for something inside the bag by the light of a hurricane lamp set on the ground. Stearman, feeling sick and dizzy from the blow to his head, swayed a little and braced his feet on the flintstone path to give himself stability. In the dark, the jumble of tombstones looked like crooked, broken teeth.

'How many are buried here?' he asked in a hoarse, broken voice. The colonel hadn't heard him approach and got up, stiffly, with a glance over Stearman's shoulder to see if anyone else had come with him.

'Oh, quite a few,' he said. 'I even spoke a few words of comfort over some of them.' Like Stearman he was dizzy and also fighting a loud buzzing in his ears. Stearman was gratified to see that his nose was broken. The bridge was swollen and both his eyes were beginning to blacken. He moved to one side, leaned both elbows on a gravestone and spat some

145

clotted blood on the ground.

'You know, John, since you came here you never lifted your head, hardly made a friend, kept to yourself. Then all of a sudden you started making a damned nuisance of yourself.'

'You knew who I was from the first,' Stearman stated.

'Parry didn't recognize you but I did. I was inclined towards the old adage that a man should keep his friends close and his enemies closer. Besides, you were a damn good carpenter.'

'You know, I think I may have made my last coffin,' Stearman told him, thinking of Lisbeth.

'I'd have to agree with that,' the colonel said, and smoothly drew a gun from his coat pocket; Stearman's own Navy Colt. 'Sorry, John. I like you, damned if I don't, but I never let sentiment get in the way of business.'

Almost simultaneously three things happened. Bell pulled the trigger, Stearman threw himself to the right behind a tombstone and something struck the colonel in the back. He gave a soft grunt and twisted, trying to reach the knife that had pierced him and was still embedded just below the right shoulder blade. He tried to raise his gun hand and managed to fire one wild shot in the general direction of the man who'd thrown the knife, but the nerves in his wrist had gone and the gun fell from his hand. He sank to one knee, a look of outraged surprise on his face as Stearman came out from behind the tombstone and bent to pick up his gun, his eyes searching for whoever had thrown the knife.

The man who walked out of the shadows was not very tall, was very spare in his frame and had dark hair, dark eyes, and was dressed in a plain brown coat and pants. He wore no hat. He came right up to the colonel and pulled his knife out with a painful twist which must have hurt like hell; it caused Bell to sink down on to one hip with a groan. He raised his eyes to look at the new man and stared as if at a ghost, recognizing him even in the dim lantern light.

'We hung you,' he rasped. Stearman looked again at the stranger. He took a step nearer, struggling to focus his eyes. It was the Rebel soldier they had brought into the woods to hang and who had shouted a warning to Hobie.

'You tried, you murdering bastard,' the man said, his voice soft with menace. 'You used to preach the Christian message, Bell, so I guess you must believe in miracles. When your comrades yanked on that rope, I prayed for God to spare me so that I could find each and every one of you. The rope must have broke because when I came to I was on the ground. You were worthless as a preacher and even more worthless as a soldier. You couldn't even hang one man and get it right. All you were ever fit for was hurting women and children, anything that couldn't fight back. You're nothing but a rapist and a filthy coward.' The stranger spoke quietly, without any rancour, but his eyes burned, incandescent with something that went beyond hatred, beyond reason.

'You killed the rest, the Rawls and Sergeant Parry?' Stearman asked him.

The stranger turned his head jerkily, having forgotten Stearman was there.

'And Phil Hunter. He was first. He raped my mother. He was easiest to kill. When I showed up he had some kind of fit and fell down dead.' He nodded towards Bell. 'My sister was hiding in a closet when they set the place on fire. I buried them next day, what was left.'

'He'll hang. I'll take him to the sheriff,' Stearman assured him but the stranger shook his head and gave a wintry smile.

'Hanging would be altogether too good for him, sir,' he

said, shaking his head almost sadly, and Stearman knew what he intended to do. He had a brief argument with himself along the lines of what was civilized and what was fitting. His father had fought all his life to bring justice to life's victims and his teachings and precepts were deeply ingrained in him, but there were a half-dozen dead girls in this cemetery and probably uncounted others, in unmarked graves from here to the coast. What justice for them? Stearman put up his gun.

'I'm sorry, I don't know your name,' he said.

'It's Kirby. Hugh Kirby.'

'Don't do this, Hugh. Let me take him in. Let the families who've lost kin find out what happened to their girls.'

'You can tell them what happened, Major. No, I want to take care of this by myself, if you don't mind. Like to thank you for trying to stop my hangin', though,' he said, and Stearman nodded. He looked down at the colonel, who had sunk down flat on the ground, bleeding heavily and aware that his hour had come, but still hopeful that something would pull him out of the fire.

'For God's sake, John, don't leave me here with this madman. I'll face what's coming, but not with him.' Stearman tried another tack, trying to read the other man's face.

'This isn't just about your loss any more.'

Kirby turned his head slightly and the light from the hurricane lamp gave his eyes a yellow gleam.

'Then whose?'

'The dead girls. What about justice for them? He needs to go on trial for these crimes, Hugh.'

'But I've killed too, in cold blood and without remorse. Revenge, you know, in law, is no justification.'

'I know,' Stearman said. 'You don't have to be here when

I take him in.'

The other man was still for a long time, then he put up his gun and nodded.

'All right, Major. Help him up.'

Which was easier said than done. Some of the fingers of Stearman's left hand were broken and it was agony when he tried to use them. He inched an arm around the colonel and braced him against his own bent knee, easing the dead weight of him on to his feet. Tiny spots like fly specks danced in front of his eyes and he felt the clamminess of an imminent faint come over him.

'Can you lend a hand?' he asked. He started to look over his shoulder at Kirby just as the flat of the shovel swung out of the dark. He heard the sound it made but felt no pain, simply dropped with a stomach-twisting lurch into complete darkness, but a soft, velvet darkness and a welcome rest. Kirby looked down at the colonel like a man examining excrement on his boot sole.

'What kind of filth are you that rapes and kills little girls?'

'The kind that enjoys it, I guess,' Bell said, defiant now, ready to do some lasting hurt before he died. 'I enjoyed your mother, don't get me wrong, but your sister, she was something special.'

Kirby's face hardened. He'd expected something like this, but it sliced into him like razors.

'Oh, you thought she hid in the closet? I put her in there to shut her up, after me and Parry took turns on her.'

Kirby gripped him by his long, luxuriant hair and dragged him to the grave, then kicked him into it. He tumbled and rolled and landed hard on the knife wound in his back. The first shovel load of dirt cut off his cry of pain and before Bell could spit out the soil in his mouth, another dozen had come down on him. The only sounds in the graveyard were of Kirby's spade shovelling dirt, the ring of the blade as it occasionally struck a rock, the soft thud of the soil hitting the body, the buried man's desperate cries becoming muffled under the weight of the dirt. Then abrupt silence.

Stearman awoke to the sound of Doc Moss gently coaxing him to take a drink from a flask he held. It was neat bourbon and it revived Stearman enough to let him rise up to a sitting position. Doc crouched beside him, his hand resting on the back of Stearman's neck, gently massaging.

'Take your time, son.'

'Where did you come from?' Stearman asked, then frowned, thinking he had said that already tonight.

'Oh, let's just say I had a hunch and leave it at that. That young fella back there, the one you thought was dead, Hobie, he said Jumper tried to kill you. And young Lisbeth is laying dead in one of the coffins. God, I'm sorrier than I can say, boy.'

The reminder of Lisbeth hit him with fresh grief, shocking, breathtaking in its intensity, but he managed to put it to one side, just for now, and tried to tell the sheriff as much as he knew.

'Barclay is Quartus Bell. He and Jumper have been luring girls from Canvas Town and sometimes getting them alone on trains, killing them, burying them in whatever grave had been dug that day.'

'What about little Betsy?'

'She's dead too. She's in here somewhere.'

'Did they kill Randall Anderson and the Rawl brothers too?'

'No.' Stearman shook his head and made a move to get to his feet. The sheriff's two deputies, the two big ones, stepped out of the gloom and helped him up. 'There was somebody else here tonight, a man called Hugh Kirby. The last time I saw him he was about to be hung by Colonel Bell's men. He's killed everybody from the ferry, excepting me and Hobie.'

'Where is he now?' the sheriff asked. Stearman took a couple of steps and looked down at the part-filled-in grave.

'He's gone. But if you want to find Quartus Bell, better have your boys start digging.'

Stearman turned away and he didn't look back as he walked a little unsteadily amongst the gravestones, heading back to the workshop.

At the door Stearman stopped and bowed his head, the bitterest and most unbearable grief swamping his senses, monstrous in its intensity and depth. How could he live with himself knowing that little girl had been abused and murdered by these men, practically under his own nose? He tracked back over the last week, trying to find a chink of light, something that would absolve him from her death, but without success. His actions had led to this and he would need to swallow it somehow.

He went inside. The candlelight softened the scene a little: the coffin on the bench and the young man standing beside it looking down, his thick fair hair hanging over his forehead. He turned to look at the man he would always call Major and he gave a slow smile.

'She's still alive, sir,' he said.

CHAPTER 24

The little party that gathered in Doc Moss's kitchen that night was a subdued one. There was no triumph at the capture of Jumper or the death of Harry Barclay, no celebrations over the discovery of the killers of Betsy Ross and at least a half-dozen others, just a tired relief that it was over. Lisbeth was unharmed, in fact she had little recollection of what had happened to her, and John Stearman was alive. They'd had a close brush with evil tonight, with a malign force that had almost taken their two lives, and they were sobered by it.

Doc's housekeeper, Mrs Terrell, had hurried across the street to see what was amiss when she saw the lights and activity in Doc's house so late at night. She took charge, cleaning the ugly wound on Stearman's brow, which had swollen and blacked his eye. She said it required a stitch or two and pulled the wound together with boiled thread from her own work basket. She made three neat little sutures that would leave only a bit of a scar, saying that any housewife worthy of the name could stitch better than old Doc Harmon. She also bound three of the fingers of his left hand together to splint the fingers that Jumper had broken.

Lisbeth she petted and fussed over, putting salve on the

bruising to her face and sending the boy Hobie back to her kitchen to fetch the leftovers of chicken pie from her husband's supper, along with fresh bread and a Dutch apple cake. At Mrs Terrell's prompting, Lisbeth told her story. She sat with arms folded, a strand of hair stuck to her cheek, her eyes hot and troubled.

It was not Mrs Joe who had struck her but Clem Stone, one of the tenants on the second floor, she told them in a voice that sounded pathetically young. He had wanted to show her something, inside his room, but Lisbeth had balked at that.

'You told me never to go in any of the rooms if the gentleman was still inside,' she reminded Stearman, who nodded gravely, glad she had remembered his warning. When she tried to leave, Stone had grabbed her and when she'd struggled he had hit her, harder than she had ever been hit in her whole life, she said, shaking her head. At this point she found her hand being held by Hobie. He gave it a squeeze and Lisbeth stared at him before she continued.

She said that Mrs Joe had come on the scene and instead of being mad at Clem, she had taken his part and admonished Lisbeth for talking back to her guests. If Mr Stone wanted her to go into his room, then next time she had better do like he said because she wasn't about to lose a good paying customer. It was time Lisbeth learned what was required of her if she wanted to keep her place.

Lisbeth had understood exactly what that meant. Mrs Joe wanted her to be . . . but she couldn't say the words out loud. She slipped her hand away from Hobie, gave him an apologetic look, then turned to Stearman, whose face was black as a thundercloud.

'But I guess I'll have to go back. I haven't got anywhere else——'

'You won't be going back,' Stearman got out of a throat thickened with rage; his one good hand making a fist under the table. 'I'm sorry, Lisbeth. I should have listened to you the other day,' he said, recalling how she had warned him Mrs Joe would find a way to get back at her. 'You don't need to go back,' he finished gently.

She had run out of the rooming-house to the hotel to find Miss Milton, but she wasn't there, so she had gone to the workshop, but Mr Stearman wasn't there either. So she had sat down to wait, and being so tired from an early rise that morning, fell asleep. When she woke the gravedigger was sitting opposite her, Mr Jumper. He seemed kind, concerned for her and offered to light the stove and make her some coffee. He neglected to tell her Mr Stearman didn't work there any more. He made the coffee and sat talking to her for a while and that was the last thing she remembered till she woke, lying in the coffin with Hobie looking down at her.

While she had been talking, she had looked around at everyone, at Doc sitting in shirtsleeves at his own kitchen table, and Mr Stearman, being tended by Mrs Terrell; but mostly she looked at the fair-haired boy, who had lifted her out of that coffin as if she was a baby, and had stayed close to her all the way back to Doc's house. He was as strong as Mr Stearman and he had a good face.

'Most girls would've been scared to death, crying and carrying on. But you were more worried about the major,' Hobie said, smiling at her, and she smiled shyly back.

'Well, you were in a terrible state,' she said, turning back to look at Stearman, at the face she had come to love and care for more than any other; his kindness, good humour and protectiveness provided the only friendly support that she had ever known in her unhappy young life.

154

'He's all right, Lisbeth. He's got a good hard head on him, no lasting damage done,' Mrs Terrell announced.

'You'll never know how glad I was when Hobie said you were alive,' Stearman admitted. Not only alive, he thought, but apparently untouched by Jumper or the colonel. They hadn't got round to that when Stearman turned up.

Hobie stood up to go just then. Doc Moss had offered him a bed for the night and he wanted to fetch his stuff from the rooming-house he had checked into earlier this evening, before it got too late. Lisbeth hesitantly got up too, unsure of her welcome, and she walked with him to the door.

'Times like this I'm glad we never had girls, me and Mary,' Doc Moss observed.

'If they'd done anything to her, if Jumper had touched her, you wouldn't need a hangman, though you might still need one when I get through with Mrs Joe,' Stearman told him.

'Don't worry about Dora Forbes, John. I'll take care of her.'

'And I'll take care of Clem Stone,' Stearman promised grimly.

'Forget about that for now. I want to know what happened tonight. What led you back to the cemetery? I knew you were holding out on me, knew it in the jailhouse. How long have you known it was Jumper?'

Stearman tried to marshal his disorganized thoughts.

'Not sure exactly. He took some things out of his pocket the other day and he had a little key with all his stuff, but it took me a while to remember where I had seen it before.'

'Where?'

'Around Betsy Ross's neck that night on the train. It wasn't till I went to Lydia that I thought of it.' It had been Cathy and her trinket box that jogged his memory. 'Then I spoke to the caretaker of the rooming-house where Tipper lodged. He told me Tipper didn't care for girls, if you take my meaning, so I asked myself what his assault on Betsy on the train was all about. When I spoke to him tonight he told me it was Jumper who'd asked him to rough up the girl on the train. Harry Barclay was supposed to get on and rescue her, befriend her and take her somewhere he could kill her. To help out his old friend Sergeant Jack Parry.'

'Speaking of trains, that girl who went missing in Lydia, the girl on the flyer? She turned up today. Sheriff Grover there in Dansing sent out wires to let a few of us know. She ran off with some young fella, then thought better of it and went on home.'

'Thank God she didn't meet Jumper or Barclay. Though if I hadn't seen that handbill I wouldn't have spoken to Tipper.'

'If I was superstitious I'd almost believe something guided you to it.'

'Pity that something didn't guide me to look out for Betsy Ross that night.'

'You're absolutely sure she's dead?'

'Jumper admitted it. Where they put her I don't know exactly. They kept the dead girls somewhere till there was a burial, then waited till nightfall to put the body in with the fresh coffin.'

Stearman became aware of a sudden silence in the room and he looked around to see what had caused it. Grace Milton stood in the doorway, flushed from hurrying across town after hearing a rumour in the hotel about what had happened. Her eyes were wide with shock. Stearman got up to go to her, taking her by the elbow and steering her out on to the back porch.

'I'm sorry, Grace,' he murmured.

'I knew really. I knew she wouldn't have run off, not Betsy.' She began to cry. He turned her towards him and gathered her into his arms, pressing her close to him, containing her grief. When her sobs slackened a little, she looked up at him. For the first time she noticed the damage to his brow, the other bruises and the strapping on his hand.

'You've been in the wars,' she said in a voice still thready with tears.

'Just a minor skirmish. The other man needed a doctor. I got by with Mrs Terrell.'

'Is Lisbeth all right?'

'She's fine. She tried to find you at the hotel but you weren't there, unfortunately.'

'I was there. Henry Johnson sent Lisbeth away without fetching me. You remember the clerk on the desk who kept watching the clock? He'll be sorry,' she said darkly.

Stearman dipped his head, lightly kissed her and everything stood still, even Stearman's heart for uncounted seconds. He gazed at her and blinked, like a man waking from a long, deep sleep.

All through the war all he had wanted was to be able to get home to his family, had prayed for it. He had walked the tightrope of danger and uncertainty every day for almost four years and got through it, not unscathed because no one remained untouched by those years, but he had kept his footing right to the end. But when he had come home to find all his family dead and Clare lost to him, he had fallen into an abyss so deep and dark he had been unable to find a way out. Now he felt as if the past had loosed its hold on him, let him take a step forwards, towards the light, towards some kind of a future. Maybe he had finally come home.

Grace put her hand up, cupped the good side of his face and kissed him back, her eyes sparkling with tears. He gave her one of those long, intense, burning looks that made her feel weak and absurdly happy, then turned his face into her cupped hand and kissed the palm.

'Don't go, Grace,' he said softly.

'I . . . I won't,' she said, but she knew he meant something more than the words.

'Go in and see Lisbeth and Doc Moss, Mrs Terrell's here. She's brought enough food for a regiment. I'll be there in a minute. Then I'll walk you back,' he murmured close to her ear. She slipped out of his arms, looked at him with eyes full of surprise and wonder for a minute, then went inside. He heard her make some pleased remark on seeing Lisbeth.

He had told Harry Barclay that he had made his last coffin and he meant it. He'd have to find another occupation now, because shortly he was going to have a wife and a foster daughter to care for. Lisbeth would be his responsibility now, until she was old enough to marry or even if she never married. Maybe they could move in with Doc Moss for the time being, for as he looked back into the warmly lit kitchen, he could see the sheriff had a contented look on his face at having a houseful of people again.

He heard a step behind him and turned as Hobie walked out of the darkness, carrying an untidily wrapped bundle.

'How's the head?' Hobie asked, indicating Stearman's freshly stitched wound.

'It's going to hurt like hell tomorrow,' Stearman admitted ruefully.

'It's good of the sheriff to let me stay here,' Hobie said and then, with a furtive glance towards the house, he spoke low. 'Lisbeth asked me to get her things. I spoke to that woman: Mrs Joe? She let me pack everything up but this got broken.' From the little bundle he was carrying he held out the china kitten, smashed into three pieces. 'I swear she did it deliberate, sir. She held it out to me then let it drop. And she tried to make me pay for my room, even though I had only been in it five minutes. She's a piece of work, sir.'

Stearman looked at the kitten, twenty-five cents' worth of cheap porcelain, but it had meant the world to Lisbeth.

'As long as this is all that got broken tonight. I'll get her another, anything she wants. And don't worry about Mrs Joe. Sheriff Moss means to take her in hand. I didn't get the chance to say it to you before but I'm glad you're alive too, Hobie.'

'Yeah, but it's hard to be alive when nearly everybody else is gone,' the young man reflected soberly. Stearman had never felt so keenly his own loss as he did at that moment, standing beside this boy who had lost as much, if not more, than he.

'I know,' he said quietly.

'I've been thinking about leaving Lydia for good, make a fresh start somewhere else.'

'Why not? Why not try here? Randolph's not such a bad little town. I think you could make some new friends here.' Stearman nodded towards the house and the young girl seated at Doc Moss's kitchen table, eating and talking cheerfully between mouthfuls to Doc and Grace and Mrs Terrell.

Hobie stared at her, then looked down at the little broken kitten in his hands. He nodded to himself, as if he had made up his mind about something, and moved towards the kitchen. He dropped his own bundle at the door and then turned and looked back at Stearman.

'I might just do that, sir. Oh, and, Major, I brung somebody to see you. Just out yonder.' He pointed to the back of the yard and Stearman turned to look, puzzled, wondering who it was. He started to move cautiously down the two steps and walked a few paces into the yard until he sensed something ahead of him, a darker shadow in the shadows of the garden, something that suddenly moved and came towards him. He heard a familiar whuff of pleasure, brought his good hand up and felt a velvety softness. Then the kitchen light fell on one large, gentle, brown eye. John Stearman gave a soft laugh and said her name.

'Bella.'